GLAMOUR LIES

JESSICA LYNCH

Callie made it five months before she could no longer pass off her bump as a really bad bloated sitch.

She'd always been on the petite side, so it was actually kind of shocking that she had managed to hide it for as long as she had. The fact that it was late January helped. Between her thick winter coats and her oversized sweatshirts, no one had any idea that she was pregnant.

And, yeah, that was definitely on purpose. So was feigning tummy trouble whenever Buster showed up at his shop, eyeing the slight bump beneath her uniform tee. Looking back on it, it was a good thing that her roommate hadn't moved back to the apartment during the early weeks otherwise she was sure Mitch would've wondered about her infrequent bouts of morning sickness. To anyone else, she might've been able to play it off as a hangover, but Mitch would've known better. Even before she got knocked up, she rarely drank. Now, no matter how much she had the urge, she refused to touch the stuff.

Bad enough her child was half human, half... *not*. What would booze do to the baby?

No. Though she allowed herself to gorge on ice cream until it got too chilly out to enjoy it—and then, courtesy of her sweet tooth, she started craving gourmet hot chocolates instead—that was her only indulgence. Doctor's orders. Before the most recent ultrasound revealed a few... quirks, she'd gone to every appointment religiously, doing everything she could as an expectant single mom. From the prenatal vitamins to upping her water intake to eating a diet high in fiber, fruits, and veggies, she was determined to do right by her baby if only because it was just the two of them.

Or, at least, it would have been if Mitch hadn't moved back to the city.

When he first reappeared, apologizing for the way he abruptly left and begging to be allowed to move back into his room, Callie didn't know what to do. At the time, she naively chalked up her nausea as an aftereffect of a human visiting Faerie; it took way too long before it dawned on her that pregnancy was even a possibility. Then, when she finally broke down and took the test, later having the results confirmed by her doctor, she couldn't figure out how to tell Mitch.

What could she say?

"I fell in love with one of the fae, he knocked me up, then dumped me"?

It was the truth, but knowing Mitch, he'd be on his fancy work cell phone in seconds, concern for her causing him to report her erratic behavior to her family back home. Even if she hadn't let on that she could still see through a faerie creature's glamour in years, her parents and her sisters had never stopped worrying over her.

And if they discovered that she allowed herself to be seduced, then discarded by one? Well, at least they couldn't deny that she wasn't just the poor victim of an overactive imagination anymore.

Nope. She was just the victim of a callous, cold fae who made her believe he loved her, too, before he sent her away from his sight...

You can't forsake what you never wanted.

That's what he had said, and for five months she couldn't get the icy sneer out of her head. Even worse because she knew he *meant* it.

The fae can't lie—but glamour did. Glamour lied all the time. Callie knew that better than most. She'd spent weeks convincing herself that her gift—her life-long ability to see through the thickest of glamour to the faerie creature hiding underneath—had blinded her to the truth: that glamour lies, the fae can't, but she'd been a fool to trust Ash regardless.

Once she confirmed that, rejected or not, their break-up didn't change the fact that he'd left a bit of himself behind when he returned to Faerie, Callie made a conscious decision to keep the truth to herself. Obviously, she'd have to own up to it eventually—kind of difficult not to when she had a baby bouncing on her hip—but she figured she had some time.

And she did. She had a little more than five months since she conceived—three months since she ran down to the drug store and bought the pregnancy test— before someone finally pointed out her noticeable belly.

Of course it was Mitch.

And because it *was* her best friend, he did it in the most Mitch way possible when he said, "Jeez, Cal. Maybe you should lay off the sugar. I still love you, but that pooch you got going on... be careful or the neighbors are gonna start thinking you're pregnant and I'm the daddy."

He was teasing. She knew he was. That was the kind of guy Mitch was. He poked and he teased, but he was always the first one in her corner. He'd been that way for years, ever since they met when Callie's older sister Ariadne started dating Mitch's older brother Tony. The two were married now, and though their families seemed sure that Mitch and Callie would eventually wise up and realize that they were made for each other, the pair were just friends. Best friends, but that was all.

So the idea of Mitch being her baby's daddy? It was clear he was only saying that to get a laugh out of her, especially since it was equally as obvious that he never for a second actually believed she was really pregnant. It was a joke, but no one was laughing when Callie stared at him in shock, unable to hide her stunned reaction to his comment.

Without meaning to, she totally gave it away.

Beneath his styled blond hair, Mitch paled. "Holy shit, Callie. You *are,* aren't you? What— I... *how?*"

It took a few seconds for her to recover, and by then she knew it was too late. She could lie—but, honestly, she didn't really want to. Maybe she had hoped that she could conceal her pregnancy just a little longer than she had, but she'd been dying to talk about it with someone. Who better than Mitch?

A tiny smile tugged on her lips. "Oh, come on. With all those different girls I see you bringing home on the weekends, you of all people should know how something like this happens."

"Well, yeah. I *know*, but, holy shit, Callie. Sure, I might bring my dates here sometimes, but what about you? You haven't been sneaking around on me, right?"

"Uh..."

"I mean, unless you're the second coming of the

Virgin Mary or something, you can't expect me to believe you got like this yourself."

Her smile faltered. While it had been a weight off of her shoulders to finally admit the truth to her roommate, that didn't mean she was ready to talk about Ash to anyone.

It had been five months since her fae returned to Faerie. A little less than four since the last time she desperately tried to summon him. He was nothing more than a painful memory.

"Mitch. I don't think—"

"Who's the father?"

"Huh?"

"I said, who's the father?"

It was the tone that had the remains of her smile fading completely. It went from a joking remark to a bewildered command to a... a *demand* so suddenly that Callie was surprised she didn't get whiplash from it.

She rested her hands on the bottom swell of her belly as she pursed her lips, both unable and unwilling to explain.

She didn't even have to answer, though. Even before he noticed her stubborn refusal, Mitch shook his head, then held up his hand. "Ah, hell. I'm sorry. I... that's none of my business. I shouldn't have asked."

Callie accepted his apology with a single nod.

Mitch cleared his throat. "Forget about that. But you... pregnant? Wow. Um..." Dropping his hand, he waved in the general direction of her slight bump. "I just... you're gonna keep it, right? The baby."

It was the same question that Callie had asked herself nearly two months after the last time she came face to face with Ash. With his dismissal still stinging, she'd sat on the edge of her toilet, the two lines on the pregnancy test almost mocking her, and wondered the exact thing.

It didn't take her long to know the answer to that. While some women might make another choice, Callie decided to see her pregnancy through to the end. What happened after the baby was born... well, she'd cross that bridge when she got to it. For now, she was only focused on seeing if she even made it nine months.

With a half-fae baby who already seemed more advanced that he or she should be, who the hell knew?

A deep breath, then a nod. "Yeah. I am."

As shocked as Mitch was to hear that she was expecting at all, he didn't seem even a little surprised at her answer.

Instead, he hesitated for a few seconds, falling forward on the balls of his feet as if he wanted to move toward her without actually taking a step. While still hanging back, he slowly lifted his hand.

"Can I touch you?" he blurted out.

Callie froze. "What?"

Mitch's cheeks reddened. "Your belly, I mean. Now

that I know it's not just a big lunch you got going on there, I thought..." His low voice trailed off before he shrugged. "It's no big deal if it makes you uncomfortable. Just thought I'd ask."

"Oh."

His request made a little sense. It was like when one of the dogs in the park came up to her. She couldn't resist the urge to run her fingers through their fur and often asked the dog's owner if she could. Only Mitch was asking her permission to touch her baby belly.

And why not?

Callie knew why not, and the fact that she even hesitated to tell her roommate that he could do something so simple let her know that she was still struggling more than she wanted to admit.

Those few weeks with Ash had really screwed her up. Before, she'd been choosy when it came to her bed partners, but she considered herself to be a touchy-feely person. Callie hugged her sisters all of the time when she still lived with them, and even a gentle brush of her shoulder as Buster complimented her on another perfectly composed photograph didn't register as anything other than support from someone she cared about.

And then she met one of the fae and learned all about the power of the touch. The higher races of Faerie could derive pleasure from touching a mortal for the simple fact that the fae were soulless creatures who stole a piece of a mortal's from every human they charmed into giving them permission. They couldn't just grab, of course. Callie knew from experience—Ash breaking the hand of a pushy idiot who got grabby with Callie during a matinee at the local cineplex came to mind—that a fae would be burned if they touched a human without permission. Their skin blistered and burned, just the same as if they came in contact with pure iron, and though they healed pretty quickly, Ash mentioned before that he abhorred pain.

He had tricked their first touch out of her. Believing she owed him a life debt, Callie let Ash touch her. By the time she learned the truth behind the kobold that attacked her in the park, the damage was done. Ash had touched nearly every part of her, including her heart and soul.

Fool me once, shame on you. Fool me twice...

But he *had* fooled her. He'd made her believe that they were meant to be, that they were fated, and she fell for it. She'd had twenty years of lessons she'd picked up on in how to deal with the faerie folk, and she threw them all away for a moment in the sun with her Light Fae.

Now she knew. Now she hardened her resolve, and in the months since he left, she'd fallen back to her old routine. Let a goblin or a redcap or—on one notable occasion—an oversized, rock-hewn troll clomp by her. Callie saw it all while pretending she couldn't.

She was good at pretending.

Pretending she didn't have the sight? Check.

Pretending she didn't suffer from heartbreak every moment since the Light and Dark Fae guards escorted her through the Fae Queen's crystal palace and to the portal that separated her from Ash for good? Check.

Pretending she wasn't scared out of her fucking mind to have Ash's baby on her own?

A glimpse up at Mitch revealed that maybe she wasn't as good at pretending as she thought. On his handsome face, she read concern mixed with reassurance as he lowered his hand to his thigh again.

Before she could think better of it, she stepped toward him, offering him her midsection. "Yeah. Sure. Go ahead."

He did. Laying his palm along the slight curve of her lower belly, his eyes widened when, suddenly, he jolted in place.

"It moved. The baby... it *moved*."

Holy shit. The baby did!

Slapping Mitch's hand away from her, Callie replaced it with her own. The slight flutter inside of her these last few days had been easy to dismiss as gas or nerves, but there was no denying that she felt a gentle thud just now. And for Mitch to feel it too?

"She hasn't kicked like that before," she marveled. "That's new."

She... for some reason, Callie had been referring to the baby as 'she' more and more lately. Call it a hunch, but she was almost sure that her child would be a girl, though she wasn't sure why. Or maybe it was just wishful thinking, really, that she'd have a girl to dote on instead of a little boy that would only remind her of the fae she couldn't keep herself from missing...

"It must like me," said Mitch, grinning as he pulled Callie out of her musing. "First time, you said. Right? How far along are you again?"

Good question.

It wasn't as if she didn't know roughly how long she'd been pregnant for. Considering she'd only slept with one guy in more than a year, it didn't take a genius to know that she conceived back in August.

But that was the thing. When the only guy she fucked wasn't exactly a guy but a friggin' fae from Faerie, Callie had no clue what that meant for her baby. They would be half human, half fae, and she didn't know if she would carry to full-term or not.

So far, everything seemed pretty normal. It took her longer than she cared to admit to finally put on her big girl panties and make an appointment with an OB-GYN because she was so worried that Dr. Flannigan would somehow *know* her baby was different. Of course, during her last appointment, the doctor had mentioned a few of her results had seemed a little curious, a little strange, and Callie had refused to go back for further testing.

How far along are you again?

The suspicious side of Callie wondered if he was only asking because, deep down, he was still trying to figure out who the dad was. By narrowing down the date, he might be able to get a better idea of the timeline.

It wouldn't help him. Considering Mitch moved out within days of her meeting Ash—and she was still convinced the Light Fae had everything to do with her roommate's sudden decision to return to the suburbs last summer—he never even knew that Callie was dating anyone, let alone one of the high races from Faerie.

"A little over five months."

"That far? And I'm just finding out now?"

"You're the only one who knows," she told him. "And, Mitch... I'd like to keep it that way."

That was one downside to living with someone who was technically part of the family. Callie's dad treated Mitch like the son he never had, and she knew that her mom and her sisters had no problem quizzing Mitch when it came to how Callie was getting along in the city. Her roommate had always been loyal to her, so she didn't really think she had to add that last part, but just in case...

"Of course. I'd never tell a soul if you didn't want me to," Mitch promised. Then, as if something occurred to him, he frowned. "The only one? Are you saying that even the dad—"

"Doesn't know," she said firmly. "He's not in the picture, either, so let's drop that, okay?"

His dark brown eyes seemed glued to her midsection, as if he couldn't look away now that he knew the truth. She got the feeling that he'd never been around a pregnant chick before—which, she allowed, could very well be true. Like Callie, Mitch was twenty-two and the baby of his immediate family. Neither of Callie's sisters had had any children yet, and Tony was Mitch's only sibling. Good chance she *was* the first one he knew.

"Gotcha."

"Good."

2

A hint of a smirk curved Mitch's upper lip. His dark eyes lit up. Something about his expression had Callie appreciating just how good-looking her roommate was, though maybe that was because he was still watching her belly as if it was something amazing.

"No dad, huh?"

Callie shook her head decisively.

If there was one thing she was sure of, it was that she never expected to see Ash again. She'd given up calling out for Aislinn; whether he tricked her when he told her that was his true name or not, she didn't know, but despite how many times she used it, he never appeared. In the beginning, she avoided the park and the charred tree where she first spotted Ash in his pristine white Faerie uniform, but she'd been there countless times over the last three months and... yeah. No sign of him.

Why would there be?

He'd made his rejection plain and clear. And as swayed by his charm and his persistent pursuit of her as Callie had been, she had some pride stubbornly lingering.

"No dad," Mitch repeated, "but the little guy's gonna need a role model. Someone to look up to."

Callie felt another flutter down low as her baby kicked again. She rubbed her belly. "It might be a girl, you know. Doctor hasn't told me yet."

"Girls could use a male role model, too," Mitch pointed out. "A kind of stand-in dad."

Her fingers stilled. "What did you say?"

"Before you get any ideas, I know that I can't replace him, whoever *he* is. And this isn't me making a move on you or anything. We're just friends, and I'm perfectly good with that. But because we're friends, I can't think of anyone better to help you out with it. Her," he hurriedly corrected, clearly remembering what Callie had called the baby earlier. "I can help you with her."

Callie screwed up her face, trying to understand. "Like platonic parenting? Is that what you're saying? Best friends raising a kid together?"

"Something like that."

"Mitch, I don't know—"

"You don't have to say anything now, Cal. It's just an idea. And if you want to tell people that I am the dad... I'm okay with that, too. To be honest, I think our moms will love hearing that, even if we both know it's not true."

He... actually had a point.

The biggest reason why Callie was holding off on telling her family was that she'd have to figure out some way to explain how she got pregnant in the first place. Mitch might've been joking when he called her the second coming of the Virgin Mary, but while Callie hadn't been a virgin when she met Ash, this definitely wasn't a case of immaculate conception. Her baby had a dad, but not one she could ever explain.

But if Mitch was offering...

"And you're okay with this?" Like Callie, Mitch was only twenty-two. He'd taken a knock at his job when he quit after he didn't get his promotion, but his boss was pleased with his work ethic. Maybe by next year he'll get another chance, and she was pretty sure playing daddy to his best friend's baby wasn't the life goal he had.

She'd been pregnant when Mitch moved back in, though she hadn't known it yet. Callie hadn't taken the test until more than a month and a half later, and she made sure to throw it out in the dumpster so that Mitch didn't accidentally find it in the trash. She hadn't been ready to tell him, either. Would he want to share the apartment with a baby? She'd never asked. Before Ash, children had been a "one day" thing, not a *now* thing.

Callie wouldn't blame Mitch if he decided this wasn't the lifestyle he wanted. Still, *she* wanted so badly to believe that his offer was genuine—and that's when he nodded.

"You know me. I'd do anything for you. I can be the perfect partner. An extra set of hands, and no expectations. We're roommates. Friends. Hell, you're my sister-in-law's sister so that makes us family, right? I want to help you, Callie. If you'll let me."

When he put it like that...

Callie rushed forward, throwing her arms around Mitch's neck. Even if he was only offering because she'd just casually dropped the bomb of her baby on him, she'd forever be grateful that he had.

"You're fucking awesome, Mitch. You know that?"

He patted her back as he returned her hug, laughing as he agreed, "Yup. I gotta say that I do."

———

WHEN MITCH SAID that he would be the perfect partner, she didn't know what to expect. Just the relief that she wasn't on her own for everything anymore had been enough for her to accept his offer. And if he backed out of it, that was all right.

But he didn't. He also didn't wait until Callie was further along before he started to prove that he really meant it when he said that he would do anything for her. That very night, he ran out into the snowy cold to pick her up a hot chocolate, a box of microwaveable popcorn, and three different movies from Blockbuster —and only one of them was a horror flick.

Though Mitch had been putting more than sixty hours into the office since his return, he slowly began to lessen his workload; rather than sixty, he topped out at forty-five so that he could spend more time at the apartment when Callie was home. Now that Mitch knew about the baby, she finally told her boss that, in a few months, she'd be giving birth and taking time off.

Buster's Photo was a two-man op. There was Buster, who owned the shop, and Callie, his sole employee. If telling Mitch had been weighing heavily on her, letting Buster in on the secret was just as tough. Luckily, he took it well, congratulating Callie while—thankfully— never asking any personal questions aside from if she planned on coming back to work after the baby was born.

That was Buster for you. It was one of the reasons she got along with him, even though he was older than her father. Like Callie, his life was his camera and his film and his pictures. He was more than happy to give her as much time as she needed, promising he wouldn't replace her if she didn't want him to.

And she didn't. Not only did she need the steady paycheck from working at store, but the added bonus of selling her personal shots would only help buy everything she needed to get ready for the baby's arrival.

But just because Mitch and Buster knew, Callie still couldn't bring herself to call her family and give them the news. That's where her roommate came in. Mitch was a friggin' godsend. He ran interference between Callie and her family, making sure Ariadne and Tony, Hope, and her parents all knew that Callie was doing well in the same way that, after Mitch moved in again, she had his back.

On his two days off, he went shopping with her, helping Callie slowly pick out essentials she would need once the baby was there. He rubbed her back and her ankles when they started to ache, he came home every night with another list of names—a mix of boy and girl names because he teasingly argued that he was sure she would be a he—that he thought she might like, and he made her smile when the pressure got to be too much.

Most of all, Mitch made her realize that this—all of it—was real, and that it would be okay.

He never pushed, either. Once she made it clear that the topic of her baby's father was a off limits, he never mentioned the topic again. And while he told her repeatedly that he was content with their friendship, Callie really believed it when he went back to casually flirting with her.

It was like the olden days. In fact, the only thing that seemed to change about her friend was his diet.

She hadn't noticed it right away. Before Mitch left last summer, they usually fended for themselves when it came to dinner; sometimes, maybe once or twice a month, they would trade off for take-out, but it wasn't often. After he returned to the city, clearly embarrassed that he had run off in the first place, he spent most of his time at the office. He ate there, and if he didn't, Callie wasn't good company. She cooked simple meals because she knew she had to, spending *her* time in the privacy of her bedroom as she switched between missing Ash and hated him for making her miss him.

Then, after she took that fateful pregnancy test, she couldn't even pretend that she wasn't avoiding her roommate.

Now that she didn't have to, though, she finally noticed something that she had missed before. Every time she walked into the kitchen and found him either prepping at the counter or sitting at the table, eating, it was always the same thing.

Fruit.

Seriously. In the dead of winter, when not a single one of the overpriced fruits he bought were in season, Mitch was chowing down on an apple there, a plum there, even peaches.

At first, she didn't say anything. When a majority of her diet was made up of sugary ice cream and decadent hot chocolate, who was she to judge? But she had to ask when Mitch turned down Chinese one night, then grabbing a pizza together the next, all in the name of friggin' *fruit*.

Turned out, it was his therapist's suggestion. Callie hadn't even known that Mitch had a therapist, let alone that Mitch's therapist was qualified to give nutritional advice, but her roommate told her that he'd been seeing Dr. Waylon since he came back to the city. It was on the advice of one of his co-workers, and he swore up and down that his weekly appointments had been a huge help.

She wanted to be supportive. In Callie's opinion, Mitch deserved to be happy, and if talking to this Dr. Waylon and trading pizza and burgers for oranges and kiwis did that, that was fine with her.

And it was, until Mitch got the idea that she needed even more variety in her diet.

That was her fault. She was the genius who mentioned how her OB-GYN mentioned that upping her water and her fruits and vegetables was super important. Mitch seized on that. He insisted she have a glass of water more frequently than her poor bladder appreciated, and he filled their fridge with every type of fruit and veggie he could get his hands on.

To make Mitch happy, she tried. She did. And

while she could choke down a banana at breakfast, and salads with lunch became a thing for her, she drew the line at eating a pile of fruit for every meal like Mitch. She pointedly reminded him that Dr. Flannagan also impressed that it was important to get her protein in before continuing to cook for herself.

That didn't stop him from nagging her to eat more fruit. Most nights, after he returned from the office but before they went to their separate bedrooms, he offered. To get him off of her back, she attempted to, but though her morning sickness was behind her as she headed into her sixth month of pregnancy, something about forcing the fruit down had her stomach turning.

It had been like that for weeks. Even so, when Mitch prepared her a bowl of fruit salad for desert that night, she want to show him appreciation for all he had done for her so far.

Callie picked up the fork, jabbing the nearest hunk of sliced fruit. It was an apple, she figured, and should be pretty safe.

Should be.

Not surprisingly, her stomach heaved. And though the idea of the fruit salad was as enticing as it always was, the sweet scent wafting over the bowl seeming to lure her in, her jaw clamped shut before she could even lift the fork to her mouth.

Damn it. It was happening again.

The fork fell from her hand. The metal stem clanged against the top of the table, the apple bouncing off of the tines before landing on the floor.

As Mitch swooped low to pick the piece of apple up, Callie made her escape. Shoving the bowl of fruit salad away from her, she climbed from her seat before bolting toward the bathroom.

She slammed the door behind him, then sank to her knees in front of the toilet bowl.

Of course Mitch followed her. She heard him call her name from a distance a few seconds before he was standing on the other side of the bathroom door.

"Cal?" He rapped his knuckles against the wood. "You okay in there?"

It took a moment before she could work past the sudden lump lodged in her throat enough to say, "Uh huh. I'm... I'm okay."

Good things she wasn't a fae because, yeah. Callie was lying her friggin' ass off.

The nausea had only gotten worse during her mad dash to the bathroom. Her stomach seized, her tongue going dry. If she kept herself from vomiting again, it would be a damn miracle.

Yanking her hair out of her face, she hovered over the bowl, her queasy stomach turning when the stink of stagnant water slammed into her nose. She heaved for that alone, before moaning and bracing herself on her forearm.

As she did, she thought—once again—of her baby. Would she be able to lie? With some of Ash's blood flowing through her veins, she might not be able to. For her sake, Callie hoped that she *would*.

If there was one thing she learned a long time ago it was that, sometimes, you have to lie. Without glamour or magic, it might be one of the only things she had to protect herself.

And if Mitch tried to get her to eat another piece of fruit, she'd shove it down his throat instead.

ASH STOOD three paces to the left of Melisandre's throne, two steps back, his hands folded primly behind his back, his sheathed sword hanging off of his lean hip.

She enjoyed keeping him on a short leash, choosing him to be one of six Light Fae guards that accompanied her whenever she left the queen's private quarters. As if eager to prove that she owned him completely, Melisandre hadn't punished him for his... fling with Callie by stationing him on the edge of the realm. Not at all. She preferred to keep him within arm's reach, flexing her control over him.

Like now.

Only centuries of practice kept the expression of utter distaste from his face as she perused the nobles gathered in her throne room, all come to pay homage to the all-power Fae Queen. It was another night, another ball, and if Ash had known that this was what his life would come to when he made his deal with Melisandre, he might've chosen death rather than this continued existence without his *ffrindau*.

Then again, since the queen had made it clear that to choose Callie was to essentially lead to his human mate being slaughtered in front of Melisandre's throne, Ash had had no choice at all. He'd spend the next millennia serving the false queen if it meant that Callie was safe on the other side of the veil.

In his mind's eye, he remembered the flash of pain that crossed his white-haired human's beautiful face when he was forced to act as if she was nothing to him but a diversion from his duties as one of the Fae Queen's elite guard. He couldn't lie to her—as a fae, it was impossible—but he did everything he could to push her away so that Melisandre never guessed that Callie wasn't just his *ffrindau*. She was his bonded mate, since he'd given her the final touch right before Captain Helix brought Ash at swordpoint to the queen to answer for his distraction.

For weeks in the human realm, he'd neglected his post on this side of the veil. Melisandre had ordered him to watch over one of the weak points between worlds and he had—until a lovely human with long, white hair and bright blue eyes *saw* him.

Callie was one of the *sealladh*, a human with the sight. She could see through glamour, she wasn't affected by a faerie's charm, and even his compulsion spells failed on her. And, though he hadn't believed it at first, she was his fated mate.

For those few short weeks, he wooed her and he courted her and, eventually, he claimed her. He bonded her to him, but his pride at finally getting to sleep with Callie was short-lived as the captain of the queen's guard finally figured out that he'd been busy with a human instead of doing what he was told.

Melisandre could have had him executed. Considering the two centuries she had been queen of Faerie was mockingly called the Reign of the Damned, he had expected her to. She lopped off heads as easily as she pretended to show mercy. He expected death, but what he got was infinitely crueler: a future without his mate as Melisandre left him no choice but to reject Callie after the queen used Ash's name to lure Callie into Faerie.

He couldn't save her while she was in Faerie. To give Callie a second chance at life without him, he had Melisandre send her away. And the queen did so if only because she got pleasure out of separating the two mates. Then, to make sure Ash couldn't find a way to twist out of his agreement to abandon Callie, she made him wear a pair of crystal cuffs that would trap him on this side of the veil.

As if he would've left even if he could. Chasing after Callie, if only to explain himself—and wasn't that something, a fae explaining himself to *anyone*—was only putting a target on her back. No. To keep her safe, he needed to stay away, and after a while, even Melisandre realized that.

Or maybe she stopped using the cuffs because she wanted to tempt him to defy her.

And he wanted to. Oberon, did he want to. But he couldn't. It seemed as if, after all the final touch, he owned more of Callie's soul than ever before. A formerly volatile, capricious, self-obsessed fae, Ash had something more important than his own happiness: Callie's.

So he did what he was told, even if that was standing behind Melisandre, guarding a queen he'd give anything to see deposed. And when Melisandre gestured toward a striking, dazzling Seelie courtesan with her golden eyes enticing and her dark blonde hair done up in elaborate curls, he swallowed his distaste as he knew exactly what was going to come next.

"Aislinn," purred Melisandre. "You've been working so hard lately. Why don't you... mm... enjoy the rest of tonight's ball?"

Right. As if he had the choice.

"Yes, my queen."

3

Her name was Gessamyn, but she was smart enough not to tell him that. As he disappeared his sword into a fae pocket—a clear sign that he was a soldier, but he wasn't on duty—before he took her hand and began to dance, she told him to call her Myn.

With a quick nod, he said, "Ash."

"Oh. I know that."

Of course she did. Even if he wasn't the recent talk of the Seelie Court, he'd been a fixture as one of the Fae Queen's main guard ever since he finished training at the Shadow Academy two centuries ago. Most of the queen's inner circle knew who he was.

There was a time when he would've bedded them all, too. As a soldier, the ladies of the court were eager to keep him and his comrades company, something he took full advantage of in his youth. After a while, he grew tired of them, only searching out a female when he was itching for a lay.

And then he found his white-haired human and he realized after that first touch that he'd never want anyone else in his long, long life.

Myn wasn't the first noble that Melisandre sent his way. Ever since the cuffs came off, she'd been choosing them, only giving him more freedoms when it appeared as if he was interested. So Ash did what he had to, just like how he spent the rest of that ball pretending as if any of Myn's chatter was interesting.

Hours passed and Ash was wondering if he had done enough to satisfy Melisandre and if he could excuse himself from Myn's clutches when, suddenly, the Seelie noble said something over the swell of the music that caught his attention.

"Did you hear about the halfling?"

He'd been slowly leading her toward the exit to the ballroom, eager to escape Melisandre's eye and make his escape while he could. With that one word, though, Ash spun her away, causing her to giggle coquettishly as he pulled her closer.

And if he only did so because he needed to be sure he heard her correctly, ah well. Whatever it took.

"What was that?" he murmured, ramping up his glamour. Even his true form was gorgeous—there wasn't a single fae that wasn't—but his glamour turned him from gorgeous to perfect. The way Myn's eyes lit up told him that the extra burst of magic didn't go unnoticed—or unappreciated.

She was also aware that was the first time all night she'd truly had his attention. Eager to capitalize on it, she said, "The halfling, Ash. As a human lover yourself, I would've thought you'd have heard by now."

Human lover... in the Fae Queen's Court, it was considered a derogatory term, to be called a human lover. Despite the fact that nearly every fae derived pleasure from touching a human, and most had brought a touched human to their bed before, a human lover took it one step further. It meant a fae who was willing to treat one of the mortals as an equal rather than a plaything.

Before Callie, Ash tossed the name around like many of his other soldiers did. To fuck one was one thing, but to actually care for one? Such an action was worthy of the scorn.

And then he found his mate in a human and, for Ash, the whole world shifted. Myn wanted to call him a human lover? Well, he was, wasn't he?

He let the name go, instead focusing on what was important. "Assume that I haven't?"

Another giggle. It was a struggle to keep the charming smile on his face, even with glamour.

Myn placed her hand between their swaying

bodies, trailing her nails down the front of his pristine uniform. "You know? I could go for a drink."

He raised his eyebrows. "The halfling?"

"There's an inn nearby," she said, surprising Ash that one of the Seelie nobles would know of it. She was quite right. Not too far from Melisandre's grand crystal palace, there were a few inns that were mainly frequented by the lower races: trolls, gnomes, redcaps, goblins, and more. The soldiers were known to frequent it, especially since the Seelie courtesans all had beds on the upper levels of the boisterous inns. "Buy me a goblet of fairy wine and I'll tell you all you want to know."

He'd already been intrigued as soon as she used the word 'halfling'—and for good reason, too. Ash was also well aware that the queen was still watching. Having her see him pull Myn out of the throne room by the hand would only help him. Let him think he was taking her off for a quick lay. The more he acted the part of the proper fae soldier, the closer he got to seeing his mate again.

Halfling...

As if she could sense that the promise of the story was the only thing keeping Ash with her, Myn refused to say another word on the rumors until they were seated at the nearest inn, an ale in front of Ash, a goblet of the potent fairy win in front of her.

He waited long enough for her to finish one goblet,

then take a couple of sips off her second before he said, "You were saying... there's talk of a halfling? You can't be serious. Melisandre would never let it live past conception."

"That's the best part! She knows and, so far, she claims not to be worried about it. Like she thinks the Shadow Prophecy is just ancient rubbish and nothing that'll affect her."

Now that, Ash knew, was horseshit. If Melisandre wasn't concerned about the Shadow Prophecy, she never would've forced him to turn Callie away that he had. Well, no. She would've if only because she got pleasure out of others' pain, but that didn't change his initial impression. Melisandre was desperate to keep a halfling from being born. In fact, he'd heard from other whispers that there hadn't been one born since she was queen.

Of course not since the queen confessed that she always separated any fated mates that might produce the prophesied halfling before they could bond, let alone produce the fated child.

In between sips of her wine, Myn tried to convince Ash that her sources—who couldn't be named, he noticed—were certain that there was a human female carrying a fae's child in the human realm.

He listened, but he didn't want to believe it. Ash was almost sure that, if the rumors reached the queen's ears—and, as the ruler of all of Faerie, certain fae would be tripping over themselves to tell her—he would've been the first accused. Every faerie in the Summer Court knew that Ash had been punished for sleeping with a human, but Melisandre knew for sure that Callie wasn't just a human pet. She was Ash's *ffrindau*, his soul mate, and if he had impregnated her, any child they had would be a halfling.

Half-human, half-fae, and, according to the ancient Shadow Prophecy, fated to bring about the end of Melisandre's cursed reign.

She told him herself. Right after she forced him to reject Callie with the entire Summer Court as witness, Melisandre confessed that she forced any fae whose fated mate was human to forsake them. No mixed matings meant no halflings. Without a halfling, her reign was secure—or so she believed.

Her belief was all that counted. And though Ash admitted that it was hard to interpret the lines passed down of the prophecy as anything different, just because he'd bonded with Callie, that didn't mean that their prospective children would ever be a threat to the Fae Queen. Melisandre disagreed, though, and if she discovered there was a human carrying a fae's child, she would've immediately accused Ash of being the father.

But she hadn't. Apart from how often she kept throwing courtesan after courtesan at him to make up for his loss, Melisandre was content to keep him as one of her guards. Though she no longer relied on the crystal cuffs to keep him at her side, she didn't have to. She already made her point. If Ash chose Callie over her, she'd kill her.

And if Callie was the human woman who the rumors spoke of, she'd be dead regardless.

Would Melisandre delight in rubbing that in his face? Part of Ash said yes. But the soldier who had stood behind the queen for years, who knew that a shrewd mind was hidden behind that seemingly innocent face... he thought otherwise. If she was so certain that she owned Ash, that he was never going to return to the Iron... why would she sacrifice his loyalty to her by letting him know she had his mate killed?

But if Melisandre was acting as if the rumor of a halfling was nothing to worry about, there had to be a reason. What did she know?

It all came down to the Shadow Prophecy. It had been foretold ages ago, though it wasn't until recently that it became clear that Melisandre was the ruler it spoke of; the lower races unknowingly calling her reign the Reign of the Damned cemented the fact. Because it was so old, though, most of it was hearsay. The part involving a halfling child was well-known, as was the nickname of her reign.

Was there more to that? Ash didn't know. As every instinct inside of him shouted that it was far too coincidental that another human female carried a half-fae child so soon after he loved, then lost his Callie, he knew that he had to find out.

And then, before Melisandre could beat him to it, he ahd to get to Callie.

If she was the female the rumors spoke of, she was in danger and she had no idea. No wonder the queen was so eager to pawn him off on countless other females. Ash had been sure she was testing his loyalty and his obedience. But what if she wasn't?

What if it was a distraction.

Pushing his untouched glass of ale away from him, Ash rose up from his seat.

Myn had still been talking, though he had stopped listening once he couldn't shake the realization that the human female she was disparaging was actually his Callie. Once he stood up, though, she stopped, looking up at him through the fringe of her thick eyelashes.

"Where are you going, Ash? To get more wine?"

"I could."

Because he could. Was he going to?

Hardly.

She beamed regardless, her golden eyes gone glassy. "Maybe see if there's a room available, too. Yes? I'm feeling rather... tired."

Ash gave her a tight-lipped smile.

Sure she was.

ASH COULDN'T LEAVE Myn's words as easily behind him as he did the Seelie noblewoman herself.

Though he knew she was expecting him to bring her upstairs to one of the inn's bedrooms like so many other soldiers did—like he had done himself in the time before he met Callie—he flagged down the huldra serving the tables, ordered her another fairy wine, then left before she could figure out his plan.

His intention was to go straight to the barracks and return to his room. But, for once, it seemed as if fate was smiling on him again because, as he strode down the hall, he happened upon a familiar face.

Inspiration struck and, instead of marching past him as if he wasn't there, he arrowed right for the gliding Dark Fae.

"Ninetroir. How glad I am to see you."

At the sound of his full name, Nine stiffened. Over the years, he'd tried everything he could think of to break the hold that Ash had on him. For as long as Ash had Nine's pebble in his pocket, he was owed a life debt, an obligation that the Dark Fae hated more than he hated most things.

And, considering this was Nine, that was saying something.

He'd offered a lesser favor despite the fact that the fae, as a rule, did *not* do favors. Nope. He sacrificed his true name, and though Ash accepted it, he preferred to think of it as a gift so that he could keep the pebble.

Just then, he was glad he had. What other leverage did he have to get an Unseelie to do something for him?

Though, since this *was* Nine, the fact that it was another subtle way to disobey Melisandre might've been enough...

"I thought you were still at the ball," Nine said.

Funny. Ash thought the same thing about him.

"The queen released me early. You?"

"The same. I thought I would do some reading since I was relieved from duty."

Not a surprise. When he wasn't training or on duty, Nine could usually be found in the castle library. He always said he was looking for something, but Ash never really cared enough to ask what.

Still, a fae fond of the library... just another reason why he chose the proper Dark Fae for the job.

"That's exactly what I was hoping to hear. Tell me, in your reading, have you come across the Shadow Prophecy?"

"I might have."

"The full prophecy?"

"Most of it, though I can't imagine it would be too difficult to find all of it."

Ash couldn't keep the cunning grin from splitting his lips. "Good. Do that for me then, would you?"

Nine's normally unreadable expression twitched, turning suspicious. "And why exactly would I do that?"

Ash pulled the pebble from his pocket.

"Ah." Nine's bright silver eyes swirled in sudden understanding. He nodded. "I'll see what I can discover."

Folding his slender fingers over the small yet meaningful hunk of stone, Ash returned the Dark Fae's nod.

"Do that."

4

His face as stunning as ever if purposely inscrutable, Ash cursed every soul and complication that was currently keeping him from betraying his queen and returning to his mate.

Damn the skirmishes, he silently seethed. Damn the insurrectionists, too. And damn the Unseelie rebels lurking in the darkness of the Shadow Realms.

Most of all, though, damn the Fae Queen and her perverse sense of punishment.

Once again, he was standing too, too close to Melisandre. It wasn't his choice; to keep her from going after Callie, Ash had to continue to play his part. The last thing he needed was to make the paranoid queen suspicious before he had the chance to meet with Ninetroir again. Though he had every intention of escaping Faerie as soon as possible, of getting back to his mate when he could, Ash was a soldier to his core. Walking into a situation without proper reconnaissance or a plan would only end in failure.

And this newest mission? It was far too important to fail.

There was a reason he chose Nine, and it wasn't only due to the life debt Ash held over his head. The library might've been a bust, but that didn't mean he didn't have other ways to get the knowledge Ash needed. As a Dark Fae, Nine had his contacts in the Winter Court, and since that was where the Shadow Prophecy originated in ages past, using an Unseelie was his best option. Still, Ash had known when he called on Nine that it would take some time for the younger fae to travel out of the Summerlands before he would even be able to shade-walk through the Shadow Realms. Days at least, and that was if he could take leave without first catching Melisandre's attention.

Ash used to find it interesting that she was so desperate to hide the fact that she was really one of the Unseelie, going so far as to always keep herself cloaked in glamour, but she chose to allow a handful of Dark Fae nobles and soldiers to serve her in her court. She did it under the guise that she ruled over all of Faerie which included both courts, but Ash wasn't so sure. It seemed, to him, that she paid far closer attention to the movements of her Dark Fae soldiers.

Or maybe that was just Nine.

He had his secrets. Ash knew that. He'd known that for decades, ever since he rescued the Dark Fae from being caught in the sun during a trip to the Iron. That was how Ash had earned the life debt that Nine owed him, and one that Ash wasn't above using to get what he wanted.

He still didn't know what Nine was doing in the Iron when he nearly burned up in the daylight. Even now, so many decades later, he knew that Nine was a good soldier who—like Captain Helix—revered the throne if not the queen currently sitting upon it, but that was all.

It didn't matter. With the pebble in Ash's possession, Nine was the only Unseelie that Ash could manipulate to learn more about the Shadow Prophecy before he fled Faerie. Melisandre would never let Ash leave the Summer Court, and it wasn't odd that one of the Dark Fae would request some time across the Courts' Divide to recharge his shadow magic.

Only Nine hadn't taken leave to visit the queen's holdings in the Winter Court. He'd been handpicked, along with a retinue of soldiers, to take another tour through Scáth, the largest city on the dark side of Faerie. The recent rebellions had been quickly squashed, but there were rumors swirling in Samradh —one of the Faerie prisons located deep in the

Shadow Realm—that there were pockets of fae still searching for the long-missing Winter Queen.

Morrigan had been missing from even before Oberon had disappeared. Ash had no doubt in his mind that Melisandre was responsible for both lost monarchs. After all, she took advantage to take the throne, the crown, and the title of Fae Queen, bringing the two courts together more than two hundred years ago.

Every few decades, the forgotten Winter Court rose up, searching for their true queen. But Faerie didn't whisper that Melisandre's reign was the Reign of the Damned for no reason. Using more force than was necessary, she ended every rebellion, just like she would use her soldiers to end this one.

And Nine was one of them.

So, rather than taking a quicker trip across the Courts' Divide, he was currently fighting in Scáth. Ash didn't know how long Nine would be there for, or how time was passing in the Iron. As one of the immortal faerie folk, time had never been a concern to him before—but it was now.

What if he returned to Callie only to find that years had slipped by? She would hardly change; now that they were bonded mates, her lifespan matched his, so she wouldn't age.

But did she know that?

Ash hadn't told her. He hadn't had the chance.

Right after he claimed her, Helix captured him, and he was forced by Melisandre to reject Callie.

That didn't break their bond, though. It would exist until one of them died, which was why Ash had agreed to the queen's demands. For now, he couldn't have Callie, but that didn't mean he couldn't return to her eventually. But now that the rumors spoke of a possible halfling child...

He had to go. Eventually was *now*.

Or it would be as soon as Nine came back to the barracks.

It had been weeks since the soldiers set out, Captain Helix leading the charge. Ash wasn't surprised to be left behind; not only did Melisandre want to keep him close, but the Shadow Realm weakened the Seelie soldiers in a way that the Summerlands didn't do to the Dark Fae. Captain Helix was a Light Fae, but he was determined, while Ash had always been content to guard his queen's back.

Now he wanted nothing more than to stab his diamond-edged sword into it.

Ash swallowed his sigh. Wearing another of her gauzy, lightly-colored gowns, Melisandre was now sweeping through her garden, tending to her statues. Each one was a trapped soul that had angered her at some point: former human pets she grew bored of, fae nobles who weren't quick enough to praise her, even a few of the lower races that she kept frozen for a while before she—*whoops*—tipped them over and they shattered into pieces along the crystal trail beneath her bare feet.

Her wavy blonde hair drifted behind her as she cooed at the statue of Raine, still frozen after he noticed the last time her glamour had slipped. Ash reflexively swallowed, forever grateful that moving his guard post had been his fate since it meant that he met his Callie rather than standing on a pedestal at the whim of a cruel mistress.

If it came down to it, Ash would rather Melisandre go for his head than freeze him as another of her playthings. Of course, he wasn't going to let that happen. Not to him, and not to Callie.

He needed to warn her about the prophecy. And if Nine didn't return soon, he would take the few lines that were burned deep in his memory and hope that would be enough.

As Melisandre took the next curve in the garden's path, the blades of springy blue grass brushing past her heel, Ash moved in time with Saxon to follow after her. Still a soldier, he was ever alert. Casting his gaze around, he noticed a pedestal that was newly empty.

Interesting.

He was sure it had once held one of the touched humans that Melisandre used to play with between taking another fae consort to replace Oberon.

The human was gone, though, and Ash found

himself straightening. With an open pedestal, the risk that Melisandre might decide to punish someone flippantly to take the human's place was notable. With so much at stake, Ash couldn't let that be him.

Glancing away, he stopped a split second after the Fae Queen paused. His hand immediately went to the hilt of his sword, but he dropped his arm to his side when he recognized the Light Fae now kneeling in front of Melisandre.

Captain Helix. He was back.

Which meant—

Melisandre's soft voice was strangely breathy as she said, "Captain. Tell me you return bearing good news."

Helix stood. "I do."

She clapped. "Perfect. Come. Walk with me. Tell me all about what happened."

"Aye."

With a careless wave of her hand, she released the three guards at her back. With another, she sent away the other three so that she would be alone with Helix. And why not? After all, if she wasn't safe with the captain of her guard, who was she safe with?

Ash didn't know. Nor did he care. Taking his leave of the queen and her captain, he couldn't care less what report Helix had about the uprising in Scáth. That was Faerie's problem, and he was already consumed enough by his own.

But if Helix was back? Odds were that Nine was, too.

Slipping his hand into his pocket, Ash squeezed the pebble tucked inside before heading straight for the barracks.

***

HE'D BARELY MADE it to his quarters before there was someone knocking at his door.

"Yes?"

"It's me."

Ninetroir.

Ash pulled open his door, gesturing for the Dark Fae to step inside before closing it behind him again.

Unlike the Light Fae, who preferred to wear their tawny hair long, Nine's dark curls were cropped. The points of his moon-pale ears poked through his perfect curls, his black uniform dotted with silver buttons as pristine as usual despite the long journey back to the Summerlands.

Glamour, thought Ash. Beneath the layer of magic, the uniform would be covered in travel dirt, the stink of the horses he would've ridden on clinging to his shadowy cloak. But as Nine stalked into Ash's room, he wasn't surprised that the Unseelie was glamoured.

He *was* fae, after all.

Tucking his hand beneath his clock, Nine drew it

back out, something feathered and white and folded between his long, slender fingers.

"Here."

"What's this?"

"Paper. I figured you wouldn't want it recorded in crystal," Nine said, holding the folded piece of paper out to Ash. "It's a bit primitive, but I jotted it down so that I had it right."

As he accepted it, Ash's head shot toward Nine. "You were able to confirm the—"

Nine cleared his throat, cutting Ash off before he could say "prophecy". Right. Because not even in his personal quarters were they truly alone.

With a nod, showing he understood, Nine gestured for Ash to unfold the page.

And he did.

The page was covered in ink-drawn lines, script of the old language that said:

BORN IN BOTH WORLDS.
WELCOME IN NONE.
REVELS IN
THE SHADOWS.
PREENS IN THE SUN.
A CHILD WITH POWERS.
PART HUMAN. PART FAE.
IN THE IRON SHE'S DESTINED

Ash didn't bother reading any further. A quick glance proved that the following lines were the whispers of the prophecy that he had already known—and they, like the new lines, just confirmed what he thought.

The Shadow Prophecy foretold that a halfling child —part human, part fae—would bring about the end of the Reign of the Damned. It was also why Melisandre was adamant that her subjects could play with their human pets, but they could never, ever take a human for their mate.

She was too late, though. Ash already had, and if he'd managed to get Callie with child...

His fingers tightened, unintentionally crumpling the sheet of paper.

It was confirmation, but over all a waste of time. Ash already knew that Melisandre would never allow a halfling to be born, so if the rumors were true, then she'd be searching for the nameless human female before she could ever have the chance to give birth. And while the chances that, their first time together, Ash had managed to get Callie pregnant weren't very high, there *was* a chance.

Callie needed to know. Just in case, she needed to be warned.

As if Ash needed an excuse to finally stop acting like he was prepared to spend forever without his mate.

Smoothing out the wrinkles in the paper, Ash

nodded again. It was as close to a 'thank you' that one fae would ever give another.

In answer, Nine held his hand out.

He disappeared the page into his pocket. "Yes?"

"I'll be taking the pebble back now."

The pebble wasn't just a pebble, and they both knew it. Decades ago, when Ash was guarding a point between realms, he watched as Nine tried to shade-walk from the Iron into Faerie just as the sun was coming up in the human world. But the Dark Fae had waited too long to weave a portal out of shadows. There weren't enough left for him to cross the veil and he began to blister in the sun.

For a moment, Ash had watched his struggle in mild interest, wondering how long it would take the Dark Fae to incinerate in the sunlight. To this day, he still wasn't sure what enticed him to get a closer look, but before he knew it, he was walking boldly toward the half-dead fae.

He could save him, but it wouldn't be out of the kindness of his heart. Throwing Nine over his shoulder, Ash lingered long enough to pick up a simple stone from the earth. The promise was made without even a word, the geas that Ninetroir owed Aislinn his life imprinted on a pebble the size of his thumbnail.

Ever since, Nine had kept his distance, even after he followed Ash's suggestion that he attend the Shadow Academy, then join the queen's guard. He still kept his secrets, but if there was one thing Ash knew, it was that Nine was willing to do anything to get the pebble back in his possession.

Ash cocked his head slightly. "And why's that?"

"The paper. I went to great lengths to get that for you."

"And?"

Nine rubbed his fingers together.

Ash pursed his lips. "No."

"Aislinn—"

"Did I say I would trade your debt for information?"

Nine opened his mouth. Closed it.

Beneath his glamour, Ash was sure he was fuming.

Nine was so young. And though Ash chose to sponsor him during his time through the Shadow Academy, he was still naive in so many ways.

He knew it, too, and he didn't mention the pebble again.

Instead, he pursed his lips, mirror-like eyes darkening to the color of iron. "You test me, Aislinn."

Ash was sure he did, just as he was sure that he would hold onto the geas imprinted on the pebble until he was forced to use it. There might come a time when he would need to call in Nine's debt to save a life infinitely more important to Ash.

And, for the first time in centuries, he didn't mean his own.

When it came to Callie, he would do anything. Risk anything.

Sacrifice everything.

Pay any price.

And it was time he proved that to her.

5

As soon as Ninetroir left Ash's room to return to his own on the other end of the barracks, Ash placed his thumb against the indent of his crystal doorknob. It locked with a barely audible *click*, the first time he'd dared to engage the magic since Melisandre finally removed the crystal cuffs from his wrists.

The Fae Queen didn't just rule the crystal mines that stretched for miles and miles below the Summerlands. As the current ruler of all Faerie, she was tapped into the precious stone that amplified her powers. It was why she only added more and more shards and pieces to the crystalline palace she stole from Oberon; a mighty enchantress on her own, Melisandre wielded the crystal like her elite guard wielded their swords but with even more brutal results. After all, it was her link to the magical resource that kept Faerie a mystical realm on the other side of the veil that turned a power-hungry, self-obsessed Dark Fae from the Winter Court to the heartless, cruel, demanding Fae Queen who rejected her mate for the promise of Faerie's throne.

It was no wonder she expected her subjects to do the same. Why she expected Ash to show her gratitude for sparing Callie's life in exchange for him "forsaking" her in front of the entire Seelie Court. For her ambition, she sacrificed eternity with her own mate. For her pleasure—and at her whim—any other fae should be able to do the same.

She told Ash that he wasn't the first she pushed to do it. Though it wasn't usual, there had been a handful of fae who discovered that their *ffrindau* was a human living in the Iron. Because she couldn't risk a halfling being born, she did what she had to to keep the Shadow Prophecy from coming true.

But Melisandre had miscalculated. If the rumors could be believed, she forced Ash to reject Callie too late. His mate might already be carrying his child— and as soon as the rumors made it to the queen, Callie would be in danger.

Locking the door was a risk, but one Ash had to take. Now that he'd gotten as much information about the ancient prophecy as he hoped to get, he had to go. He wasn't so naive as to believe that Melisandre didn't have eyes on him. She might have stopped trapping him with the crystal cuffs, but that was only because she got her way when Ash seemed to be interested in courting Gessamyn. She thought another female in his bed could so easily replace his Calliope, and she was wrong.

That wasn't the only thing she was wrong about, either.

Melisandre believed she was untouchable. That none of her subjects—least of all one of her hand-picked soldiers—would ever defy her. And if it had been only his head on the line, he wouldn't have. But Callie... if there was still a chance to protect her from the cruel Fae Queen, then Ash would do whatever it took to get back to her.

He gave her up once, hoping that his sacrifice would be enough to keep her safe. Well, now he knew that he let two centuries of loyalty to Melisandre blind him to the truth: that she would gleefully rip out Callie's heart and slaughter an innocent child without even blinking while expecting Ash to kiss her bloody hand.

No. In the name of Oberon, *no*.

The crystal would talk. If Melisandre was listening, she would know instinctively that Ash had locked his barracks door. He gave her precious few minutes before she sent another guard to his quarters, eager to flex her power over him.

Ash's fiery gaze blazed as he looked around the

room he'd spent centuries in. There wasn't a single damned thing he would take with him when he went and he felt... *relief* at that realization. With Nine's pebble tucked securely in the opening of his uniform pants and everything else—his wealth, his weapons, and the item he treasured above all, Callie's brush full of those white-blonde strands of hair—hidden inside of a fae pocket, he imagined the fury Melisandre would experience when she was forced to break past the crystal lock herself only to discover an empty room.

A ghost of a smile tugged on his lips as Ash lifted his hand. The wash of pleasure at just how angry the queen would be paled in comparison to the anticipation welling up inside of him. He was returning to his mate—*finally*—and he only hoped that, in the time that they'd been separated, his tempestuous human hadn't replaced that cast iron pan of hers.

Four slashes, quick and decisive. Faerie fire leapt eagerly from the tips of his fingers, from the side of his hand as he drew a doorway in the center of his room.

If giving Callie up by rejecting her was the way to save her, he'd stay behind in Faerie where he could keep his eye on Melisandre. But if the Fae Queen eventually realized that the human pregnant with a fae's child could be Callie... it wasn't the queen herself he had to be afraid of. It was her reach, including the soldiers at her command.

Staying away from Callie was leaving her wide open to Melisandre's cruelty. He couldn't have that.

He had to go.

And, knowing that Melisandre would make him pay if she ever caught him, he stepped into the portal and, following the bond he refused to forsake, headed straight for his mate.

Too bad something stopped him on the other side of the veil.

He was in the Iron. From the way being in the human world prickled at his skin like a thousand different fairy bites, to how the sky over his head was bright blue instead of a burnished magenta, Ash was in the Iron.

The tall building looming in front of him? That was Callie's building. He could sense her inside of it, almost as if the bond stretched between them was pulling him toward her. But if she was still living in the same iron cage, why hadn't his portal taken him straight to her? It always had before.

No time to waste figuring it out. After checking that his glamour was set—hiding his pointed ears, turning his white uniform into a facsimile of what a human wore—he strode inside of the apartment building.

He refused to step inside of the metal box—the elevator—that would bring him up to Callie's apartment on the tenth floor. Fresh out of Faerie, too much magic clung to his aura; using the metal box was just begging to short it out like so many of Callie's human appliances. Instead, he strode right toward the stairs, his soldier's boots pounding against the cement as he made his way to his mate.

The wards hit him when there were still a few flights to go. The invisible barrier was strong enough to cause Ash to stop mid-step, aware of the sudden buzzing in the air. It was a warning, laced with herbs and iron and salt. It wouldn't be enough to stop him, but that was only because he was a bonded male desperate to get to his mate. Any other creature from Faerie would find it difficult to fight.

Pride bloomed inside of Ash. That was his Callie. He didn't know how—and he hoped he hadn't arrived too late or that she'd had reason to learn how to protect herself on her own—but Callie had warded her home.

So what if that meant that he couldn't just appear inside of her space? At least she was safe.

For now.

And, as soon as she let him in and they were together again, he'd do whatever he had to to keep her that way.

It was only late afternoon, but Callie was already lying in bed with her feet up.

It had been a long shift at Buster's. She headed down to open the shop before eight like she usually did, expecting an easy day. It was flurrying out, though the forecast said it should clear up shortly, but it was still early February. Cold. Dreary. With the holidays long over with, and summer vacations a dream a few months away, the shop was entering another lull in the season.

Tell that to the customers, though, thought Callie as she probed her temples. It had been one headache after the other—Mrs. Wilson needed a quick turn around on six rolls of film, while Mr. Doherty wanted to know why his 50x60 poster wasn't printed and framed just yet—until Callie actually felt a migraine forming behind her eyes.

Still, she toughed out the rest of her shift, staying on well past three to give Buster a hand with the influx of orders. Grabbing a quick sandwich to scarf down, she planned on heading straight to her bedroom, showering off the day, and getting some rest.

It wasn't Mitch's day off, but her roommate was sitting in the kitchen when she let herself inside the apartment, absently munching on a pear. He motioned for Callie to join him, nodding sympathetically when she asked for a rain check. Just as well since Mitch admitted he was only home because the floor of his building was being fumigated and he had a shit ton of work left to do. As soon as he finished his snack, he headed to his room while Callie went to hers.

The nagging headache from earlier was on the edge of turning nasty. After eating her sandwich, she took a tylenol, then laid down. She was still working up the energy to make it from her bed to the shower when, suddenly, she sat up.

Why? No idea. It was like the urge to get up and pee when you were previously comfortable; it came on quick and strong and so undeniable there was the chance she could piss herself if she didn't move and now. Only she didn't have to pee, a miracle in and of itself considering she was pregnant and having to go was a pretty constant state these days.

No. It wasn't that. Without understanding why, she had the impulse to get up and go out in the hall.

Had Mitch called her? It almost seemed like someone had. Maybe she'd been too dozy to pay attention.

Swinging her feet around, she set her sneakers on the floor, wincing when she noticed that she hadn't even bothered taking her shoes off before she climbed into bed. Running her fingers through her long, white-blond hair, she fluffed it out while adding "change bedding" to her mental to-do list.

In the hall of their apartment, there was a linen closet. Might as well grab a new pair of sheets since she was already going out that way.

The moment she stepped out of her room, the bed was completely forgotten. As if she was made of metal and the front of the apartment was a gigantic magnet, her head swiveled toward her door, shoes shuffling that way before she even realized she was moving.

What the—

The air crackled. A shock jolted her arm, the pale blond hairs standing straight as she shook off the strangely uncomfortable feeling. Her stomach tightened, her jaw clenching shut as she realized too late what her living room felt like.

Magic. It felt like magic.

In Callie's experience, there was only one type of faerie creature that gave off an alluring aura like that.

She tried to stop. Tried to turn around, run back to her room, climb under her blanket and hide... but she couldn't. The pull was too strong, or maybe Callie was too weak. Whatever it was, she moved toward the front door even though her brain shouted at her to stop.

And that's when she heard his voice whisper through the door.

"Callie..."

A shiver coursed down her spine.

Aislinn.

No. *No.* He couldn't be out there. It wasn't possible. He rejected her—he basically threw her... threw what they had together... all in the name of the Fae Queen. She was where Ash's loyalty lied, not Callie.

It had finally happened. Despite all of Mitch's recent help, she'd finally lost it. She'd snapped. It was inevitable. Though she wanted to pretend she didn't, she missed Ash the way she missed the sun when the rain and the snow came. She figured the only way she'd get past losing him was by stubbornly pushing forward, but the closer she got to the end of her pregnancy, the more she secretly wished he'd come back.

And now she was imagining that he had.

Only... even through the thick wood, she felt the heat of his aura pulsing toward her. The strange tug across the apartment had led her down the hall, toward the door, and every nerve in her body was vibrating as she forced herself to stay still. Her head ordered her to freeze while her heart... her heart was outside of the apartment.

The same way it had been since Ash stayed in Faerie while Callie was shoved back through the fiery Light Fae portal.

"Callie. I know you're in there. I can sense you. Come to me."

When she first met Ash, he was such a commanding presence, nearly every word out of his mouth was an order.

He'd expected her to follow them, visibly surprised when she refused. It was a power belonging to his kind, charming and compelling humans to bend to the will of the fae, but Callie's gift made her immune.

When Ash first started to pursue her, she convinced herself that her gift was the only reason why Ash kept coming around. So unused to being told 'no', he kept coming back, hoping he could find a way to get her to say 'yes'.

And he had. She said yes, and then he was gone without ever saying goodbye.

Nope. His last words to her were so, so much worse.

You can't forsake what you've never wanted...

Turning, she placed her back against the door, leaning her head against it as she splayed her fingers against the wood. "Go away," she whispered. Mitch's door was closed and she was desperate for it to stay that way. "Just go."

He heard her all the same.

"I can't."

He had to. "*Go.*"

"No, Calliope. I won't."

Callie closed her eyes. The gentle, lyrical way he said her full name... The pinch at the back of her throat was the first warning she had. The lump lodging right below the pinch came next. Tears burned behind her eyelids, but she didn't shed them.

She didn't open her eyes yet, either.

It had been a gift. The day they spent together— the hours in bed that led her to her current predicament—had seemed so special at the time that she wanted to prove it to him. When it came to the fae, emotions were a weakness and talk was cheap. He'd already taken every last piece of her soul by the time she both accepted and seduced him, but there was one thing he didn't own.

Her name.

Callie gave him her name.

How dare he come back six months after he cast her aside and use her fucking name like that?

"Calliope." The pang hit her all the way to the depths of her heart when the bastard did it again. " There's something blocking me from getting to you. Let me in."

A laugh bubbled up her tight throat. At least that was one bit of good news.

It had been a fluke. Though she tried desperately to go back to pretending that Faerie and the fae and everything associated with Ash didn't exist, she couldn't help herself. Ever since she was a kid and realized that the things she saw—things no one else could see—were real, she'd done everything she could to protect herself, including checking out every book of myths and legends on the faerie folk she could get her hands on.

Some she bought, some she borrowed, and a few she technically stole since she neglected to return them to her local library. Her most recent one she stumbled upon in the used bookstore down the block from Buster's. But it wasn't the decades-old book with its yellowed, feathered pages that was her big find.

Nope. It was the recipe.

Tucked inside of the book's dust jacket, the recipe was written in pencil on the back of an index card. That's what it was called, too. In block letters, the words **WARDING RECIPE AGAINST FAIRIES** was printed at the top, followed by a list of... interesting ingredients.

Coarse salt. Iron shavings. Fresh ash. Daisies. Slivers of rowan. Red verbena.

Figuring, "what the hell," Callie gathered as many of the ingredients as she could find before combining them in little burlap bags that she tied with twine. Following the handwritten instructions, she hid them all over her apartment. The idea was that the pouches would act as a repellent to creatures from Faerie.

Did it work? She had no way of knowing. It couldn't hurt, though, and since she never expected that Ash would visit her again, she set the pouches out to make sure none of the vicious Fae Queen's guards could, either. Six months later and she still hadn't gotten over the shock of that Light Fae captain appearing suddenly in her bedroom. If the recipe could protect her even a little, it was worth a shot.

Mitch didn't mind. The first time he found one of the pouches that she hid in the corner of the couch, she lied and told him it was a potpourri sachet and he shrugged, shoving it back where he found it without even pointing out that it smelled more like something that belonged in a kitchen than freshening up the place.

Until now, she hadn't had another faerie visitor. She figured the recipe had to have done something, though, since Ash was on the other side of the door and he couldn't get to her.

Good. He could stay out there.

"Let me in."

"No."

She wouldn't—and not only because she wasn't alone in the apartment.

The time when she would do anything for Ash was done and over with. So what if he suddenly reappeared? He'd been gone long enough that her heartache had turned to bitterness. If it meant she never stepped foot out of her place again—turning it into a true iron cage like he had mocked her for so long ago—she would if only to avoid coming face to face with Ash.

But he was stubborn. She'd never forgotten that. An arrogant fae through and through, Ash wasn't just going to accept that.

"If you won't let me in, then come out here. We have to talk."

It was a little late for talking.

With a rueful laugh, she snapped back, "Yeah? Give me one reason why I should."

"I'll give you two," came Ash's haughty reply. "You're my *ffrindau*, and you're pregnant."

It was a blessing that Callie was leaning against the door. The way her knees went weak to hear that Ash *knew*... well, dropping to the floor couldn't be good for the baby.

The baby that her fae lover—not her *ffrindau*, she refused to think of him as her mate—wasn't supposed to know about.

6

Hoping that Mitch wouldn't notice that she was leaving the apartment, Callie grabbed her coat from the back of the chair in the kitchen, shrugged it on, then zipped it all the way up to her chin. Just because Ash had dropped the "p" word like that, it didn't mean she needed to give him visible confirmation of her growing belly.

Her hand was shaking as she reached for the first of the three iron sliding locks she'd installed shortly before Mitch moved back just in case. If her roommate thought her newfound obsession with keeping the apartment's front doors and windows secured was strange, she had spun him a story about a spate of break-ins while he was back in the suburbs and he quickly changed the subject without ever mentioning it again.

What else could she say? That she was worried about faerie creatures breaking into her home? That she was afraid they would be coming for her baby? Mitch might be willing to stand by her as a single mother, but if she ever gave him any clue what was really going on, she had no doubt that he'd be wrangling an intervention with Ariadne, Hope, and her parents before she could blink.

Speaking of blinking—

As she hesitantly pulled her door open, Callie dropped her gaze. The hallway outside of her apartment was much warmer than it had any right to be considering it was February and her landlords didn't believe in heating the communal areas. Even before she saw his pristine white leather boots, the bottom of the uniform he habitually wore, she knew that the heat pouring off of him would only belong to one male.

Don't look at him.

Don't look at him.

Don't look—

She looked.

Damn it. Why couldn't Ash have grown a third eye or developed a case of warts or something?

Of all the faerie folk she'd seen since she was small, Ash was the most dazzling and that was without any glamour at all. The fae usually wore their glamour like a second-skin, making them irresistible to their human prey, but Ash hadn't need to for Callie. She'd been snared from that first moment their eyes locked that summer afternoon in the park. Thanks to her sight, he never would've been able to charm her that way, but his appearance always stunned her anyway.

Over the last few months, she almost believed that she exaggerated his beauty. All it took was one unfortunate glimpse up at him to prove that, if anything, she'd undersold it.

She choked on a breath, forcing herself to look past the heat in his blazing, sun-colored gaze, his luxurious tawny hair, his perfect features. Only when she was sure she could speak without squeaking did she ask, "How did you know?"

So help him if figuring out he knocked a human woman up was one of his fae abilities, like glamour and compulsion... Ash was immortal, but if he knew and left her alone these last six months anyway, she'd *find* a way to kill him.

"I can't say that I knew, but I had reason to believe it was so. And now I do."

If it wasn't for the fact that they were out on the street, in full view of countless strangers, Callie would've screamed. How had she forgotten how annoyingly frustrating it was to have Ash answer one of her questions with a twisty, fae sort of answer.

Welp. He wasn't wrong, was he? Her demand had basically confirmed that, whether he was fishing or not, he'd caught a nibble when his retort had Callie rushing out of the apartment to face him. So now he knew her secret because she was the idiot who wasn't quick enough to deny it.

Would she have, though? Callie had to admit that she probably wouldn't. The way Ash said that... *reason to believe*... she couldn't let it go. As careful as she'd been to hide her pregnancy, unless Mitch or Buster went blabbing, no one should know.

Especially not someone from Faerie.

"Screw that," she said sharply. "Someone told you."

Did expect him to change the subject? Because he couldn't lie, Ash evading a topic was a clear sign that he didn't want to answer her. But he didn't do that. Neither did he continue with twisting his words.

To Callie's surprise, he actually answered her.

"Yes."

She blinked. "Who?"

"It wasn't just one person. The whole of the queen's Court has been whispering that, in the Iron, there was a human female carrying a child with faerie blood. Fae blood."

Ash's blood.

She gulped, too stunned to be worried. That, she was sure, would come later. "What? How did *they* know?"

"I can't say." Before Callie could ask why, he said, "I can't say because I don't know. I didn't want to give any credence to the rumors by acting as if they could be true."

Which, of course, they very well could be. It didn't matter that Ash decided to end what they had when it was just beginning. By the time he changed his mind, the damage had been done.

And news of her pregnancy had somehow made its way across the veil.

"Know what? Forget that." As if she could. The last thing she wanted to hear was that her baby was the talk of the Fae Queen's Court. "What's going on? You heard some poor human got herself in trouble with one of your kind and figured it might be me. So? That still doesn't explain what you're doing here, Ash."

Deep down, Callie hoped that he'd tell her that the rumors made him realize that he still loved her, still wanted her. That he heard about the baby and he was overjoyed at the news.

The way his bright eyes darkened, turning from molten gold to a burnished orange color, was the first clue that she might be standing in the Iron with Ash, but she was living in a fantasy world.

"I'm here because someone had to warn you. You're in danger, Callie. You *and* the child."

Turned out she was wrong. Because *that*? That was the last thing she wanted to hear.

She swallowed roughly.

"Explain," she said, pleased she could at least get

the one word out. Screaming was still very much on the table just then, but she forced the word out through gritted teeth.

Ash raised his eyebrows but, rather than refuse to do as she said, he conceded.

Explain? That's exactly what the Light Fae did.

As she hugged herself, trying like hell to ignore the February chill seeping through even her winter court, Callie listened as Ash told her about the Shadow Prophecy, an ancient Faerie prophecy that foretold the end of Melisandre's reign as queen.

He rattled off the lines he'd obviously memorized, but she understood why he came to warn her once she realized what the prophecy was about. It seemed as if it was foretold that a halfling female—a girl child that's part human, part fae—would overthrow the Fae Queen. And since the only way Melisandre would ever give up the throne was over her dead body, it didn't take a genius to realize why Ash thought she was in danger.

Didn't matter if Callie's baby was the prophesied child or not. A halfling was a very real threat to the cruel queen, and from everything she learned about Melisandre, she wasn't the type to sit back and wait to see if Callie gave birth to a girl.

Nope. Her M.O. seemed more like kill the pregnant lady so that the problem of the halfling went away on its own—and Ash went ahead and told her as much.

Was she scared? She probably should be. When Ash left again, and she got over the heartache of seeing him, she was sure she would be.

For the moment, though, she appreciated the heads up, even if it did come from him. Now she knew to be on her guard, so even though it was rough being so close to Ash again after so long, she didn't lash out at him like she wanted to.

He was still so cold. So emotionless. She wasn't sure if he was acting more like the fae who sicced a kobold on her as an experiment, or the disinterested bastard who sent her out of his sight. Either way, the male standing with her now wasn't the devoted, caring lover she'd fallen for.

These days, she wondered if he ever had really been. Or was it just another type of glamour? Not the type of spell she could see through because of her impressive sight, but one that tricked her all the same.

Glamour lies, huh?

He was watching her closely, unblinkingly. Tucking a strand of hair behind her ears, she purposely looked away from him, avoiding his gaze.

How long had they been outside? Long enough that she was pushing her luck. At any minute, Mitch might poke his head out of his room and realize that she was gone. And while he didn't know a single thing about Ash, what were the odds that he wouldn't take one look at the tension between the two of them and immediately figure out who Ash really was.

And she sure as hell didn't mean one of the fae.

She glanced at the sun as it hung low in the dreary sky. One good thing about it being winter: the days were shorter, the nights longer, and she could finally end this charade. Whatever his reasons for crossing back into the human world, with the sun getting ready to set, he couldn't stay.

Might as well get this over with then.

"I... I really don't know what to say except I appreciate you coming to tell me. I honestly didn't think you'd care that much, even if I am in danger."

Out of the corner of her eye, she saw Ash's jaw tighten, making the edge as sharp as a knife. "I care a very great deal, Callie."

He couldn't lie, but she struggled to believe that.

I told you what you needed to hear...

"Right. I forgot." The slight sneer was out before she could help herself. "You're just trying to protect me from that bitch— oops, *sorry*. Your queen."

You think she would've remembered just how quick he was. Before she knew it, he was *right there*.

Ash reached out toward her, slender fingers coming within centimeters of the side of her neck. A moment's hesitation, his hand hovering, then he slowly withdrew it before he could actually touch her skin.

Huh. Callie had to wonder: did the overarching permission she gave him that afternoon they slept together still count? Or any of the other times she told him he could touch her anywhere? She didn't know, and if Ash did, he wasn't giving anything away.

Even his expression went closed off as he said, "Be careful, Callie. Melisandre has eyes and ears everywhere."

And, yet, he was the one who thought it was a good idea to drag her out to a public place instead of the safety of her warded apartment. If he really pushed it, she could've relocated her pouches so that he could at least step a few feet inside—but he hadn't pushed it, and Callie did harbor any illusions that it was because he was actually thinking of her for once. Was this just another set-up? He couldn't lie, but she would never forget the cold way he made it clear that he told her whatever she wanted to hear.

Maybe he was doing the same thing now.

She didn't doubt that he was being honest. He was fae; he had no choice *but* to be honest. And he wasn't reverting to that confusing double-speak where he said one thing, meant another, and neither was a bald-faced lie. Talking in absolutes wasn't what a fae often did, but he was when he said that Melisandre would rather kill Callie now than risk her giving birth to a halfling child that could possibly kill *her*, she had no trouble believing that.

But to accept that he might actually feel something for her after how callously he dumped her?

That was a little harder.

"Good night, Ash."

He blinked. "Where do you think you're going?"

"Home. Which is where you should be going." She pointed over his shoulder. "Look. It's gonna be sunset soon." What did he use to call it? "The time of shadows. You've gotta be going. Me, too."

"Not yet."

She ignored him.

"Calliope—"

It was the name that did it. If he'd used her nickname, she might have been able to stroll right past him with her head held high. But the second she heard him use her real name, she couldn't stop herself from whirling on him.

"Don't call me that."

He cocked his head enough to be obnoxious. "It's your name. You gave it to me."

"I gave it to the man who promised me forever, not the asshole who hit it, then quit it."

The haughty fae would never admit that he didn't understand what she meant. And maybe he did since he said, "It's not what you think. What happened in Faerie... if there was more time, I could explain."

But there wasn't time, was there? The sun was setting, and even when he'd managed to convince her that he cared for her, that they were made for each other, Ash refused to stay the night no matter how much she begged him to. To retain his magic, he had to return to Faerie once the shadows came, and he always did.

Just like she was sure he would now.

There was no time, but that didn't stop Callie from shooting out one last question: "Why are you here, Ash? Why did you really come?"

"Because you're my mate. You're carrying my child. My flesh. My blood. My family."

She scoffed. "You gave that up when you dumped me in front of half of Faerie."

"I told you. It's not what you think."

"And I told you 'good night'."

Giving him as wide a berth as the sidewalk allowed, careful not to accidentally brush up against the Light Fae, she started toward the entrance to her apartment building. Right before she stepped inside, she glanced over her shoulder.

And even though he was already gone, disappearing in the few seconds she'd had her back turned on him, she still let out a ragged whisper.

"Good night, Ash. And goodbye."

SLEEP DIDN'T COME easy for Callie.

She managed to slip back into the apartment without drawing attention to her absence. Mitch's door was still closed, and she shuffled past it before sneaking inside of her room.

For the rest of the night, she tried to put her talk with Ash out of her head. Like she guessed, once he was gone, fear set in. But not for herself. Oh, no. Callie was terrified for her baby's sake, and she used the last of her supplies to build another four packets of the warding recipe that she then placed in the corner of her bedroom for added protection.

She was too nauseous to eat so she skipped dinner, even though she knew she'd regret it come tomorrow. But that was future Callie's problem. Present Callie was too busy wishing that Past Callie had never invited Ash to her apartment that fateful day in the park.

When Mitch knocked on her door later that night, checking in on her, she pretended she was asleep. She even threw in a couple of fake snores for good measure. There was a good chance he knew she was full of shit, but Mitch knew when to leave her alone. Her thoughtful roommate simply tiptoed away from her door, giving her her space.

That's when she decided she might as well just go to sleep. Two hours later, she was still awake.

Maybe that's what she got for faking. Or maybe it was because she just couldn't stop replaying every second of their interaction over and over again as if looking for some deeper meaning in Ash's sudden reappearance—and subsequent disappearance—in her life.

Finally, after she gave up on tossing and turning for the countless time, she threw her covers back and eased her aching back out of bed. Callie winced when her bare feet hit the chilly floor. Ever since she left Ash out on the sidewalk, she'd been shivering, almost as if he took every last ounce of heat away from her.

Her stomach was unsettled. Though she knew it had nothing to do with skipping dinner, she had her baby to think about. If she was up, she might as well try to get something down.

As she stepped out of her room, she had every intention to head toward the kitchen. But once she had, it was like deja vu. She had the same urge from earlier, the one that told her to walk toward the front door instead.

Callie was too beat to fight against it, especially when she noticed that she was sloughing off her bone-deep chill with every step down the hallway. Not only that, but the sensation that someone was lurking out in the hall was growing stronger and stronger as got closer to the door.

She didn't know what to expect when she peered through its peephole. This late, there shouldn't be anything. Ash was long gone, and it wasn't like they were expecting any visitors.

Still, she had to peek.

No one was there. That actually surprised Callie since she was so sure she had sensed someone lurking on the other side of the door. Then again, on the plus side, that meant that there wasn't a fae soldier waiting to attack her in the name of his queen.

Callie pursed her lip. Call her sensitive, but the feeling hadn't faded. For her own sanity, she reached for the first of the locks. If she didn't at least get a better look, she'd never get to sleep, and she friggin' knew it.

One lock. Two locks. Three.

Pulling the door in, she looked out in the hall. Nope. It was empty and—

Hang on… what the— oh.

Lying a few inches past the edge of the threshold, Callie found a single flower.

Its bloom was bright yellow, its stem thick and sturdy. Bracing her back with one hand, she squatted low, reaching for the flower with the other.

She recognized it immediately, and what it meant.

A freesia bloom, Ash's way of reminding her that his was an unconditional love.

And its stem was still warm from his touch…

Even though she refused to brush up against his skin earlier, Callie could sense his aura lingering on the stem. She couldn't explain why, only that she was certain of it.

Just like she was certain that he had left it for her.

Only... only it was well past midnight. The sun had set hours ago, shadows filling the empty hall. None of Ash's kind would choose to stay in the human world once night fell. Even when they were still together, no matter how much she begged and how he had seemed like he wanted to linger, Ash always left while there was still some light out. If he didn't, he'd trade his fae magic for iron sickness. He'd grow weak, losing his color first, his tether to Faerie next. To stay in the Iron as one of the Light Fae was to turn his back on Faerie. It wasn't quite a death sentence—not like it was for a Dark Fae caught without any shadows to protect them —but it was close.

Callie twirled the stem between her fingers, her heart racing as her exhausted mind tried to fight past what Ash's gift could mean.

Unconditional love from a fae

It meant he wanted her back.

She gulped.

He wanted her again. And, remembering how he claimed her baby as his child, she realized that he wanted their child, too.

He wanted his family.

Maybe it wasn't goodbye after all.

7

B ut it had to be, right?

That's all she kept thinking about as she re-engaged all three of her locks before returning to her room. That this had to be Ash's way of saying goodbye, only... what would he bring her the freesia?

He'd done it once before. Last summer, when Callie discovered that Ash was responsible for the kobold that tried to attack her, she was so pissed off that she kicked him out of the apartment. It was like a slap in the face. After spending weeks naively believing that Ash was being honest with her because he couldn't lie, she was hurt to learn that the Light was just as tricky as the rest of his kind.

He hadn't understood why she was so upset. The way he saw it, he'd changed his mind about using the kobold against her as soon as he released it from his burlap sack. He burst past the veil, skewering the beastly creature with the tip of his sword before he could get a single one of his sharp teeth in her. That should count for something.

Not to Callie.

To her surprise, it seemed to hit him after she threw him out of her home. And even if he didn't, he made an attempt at apologizing. Instead of returning to Faerie, he left to let her cool off, then came back carrying a bouquet of flowers.

They were freesia, he told her. When she made a jab that he could've at least brought her roses, Ash had sneered. Anyone could say "I love you" with roses, but the freesias meant he loved her unconditionally.

And now he had brought her another one, months after he dumped her.

What the hell was *that* about?

After hiding Ash's flower in the top drawer of her dresser, beneath a stack of dainty panties she hoped to fit into again one day, Callie dropped onto her bed and cupped her chin with her hands.

Okay. Forget what her fae wanted. What did *she* want?

And when the hell had she started to think of the jerk fae who abandoned her as hers again?

Ugh.

To think that she believed sleep was hard to come

by before she realized that Ash was sneaking around outside of her apartment. He should've been back in Faerie by now, but unless someone else just so happened to know to drop the yellow flower in front of her apartment while also making her sense a Light Fae's aura, it *had* to be Ash.

But *why*?

That thought kept her up later than she wanted to admit. Or maybe it was the way she had her ear cocked, her senses reaching for Ash. Would he come back? Had he even stopped by in the first place?

All good questions and, the next morning, Callie woke up before Mitch did in the hope that she could get the answers to them. She shrugged on her coat, thinking that her best bet was to start at the park where she'd first seen Ash.

That was the downside to having a fae for an ex. It wasn't like she could just call him on the phone to get a hold of him. And, sure, she could try shouting out his true name, but after it had failed so many times before, she had a knee-jerk reaction to keep it to herself.

Maybe later. First, the park.

Tiptoeing past Mitch's room, she thought about leaving him a note but decided against it. He had work in two hours, and if he wondered where Callie was on her day off from Buster's, she could always tell him that her boss called her in last night.

Anything was better than admitting she was

looking for the male who knocked her up and got out of Dodge before he ever had the chance to figure it out.

But now he knew. Would that change things? He'd warned her that she was in danger. Callie had no doubt that that was true. Then again, she'd been in danger her whole life courtesy of her gift. Hopefully, she'd find a way to use it to save her baby. And if it meant relying on a fae soldier protector?

He used her once. It was about time she returned the favor.

And she had that thought in mind for about, oh, fifteen seconds? Because that was how long it took for Callie to hook her purse past her wrist, unlock the door, and slip outside only to come face to face with Ash.

He had his back against the wall opposite of her door. The faint haze surrounding him told Callie that he was wearing a heavy dose of glamour—in case he ran into one of her neighbors, probably—but she could see right through it.

Oh.

She didn't ask what he was doing out there. It was obvious. Almost as obvious that her suspicions were correct.

He never returned to Faerie yesterday evening and, for the first time, Callie finally understood why it was so important for the Light Fae to leave once night fell.

Already, Ash looked super different. His bronzed

skin had faded, his bright eyes losing some of his shine. He had dark circles under his eyes that she'd never noticed on her fae before.

"You didn't return to Faerie."

It was a statement.

"If I didn't make it clear to you, that was my fault. I've returned for you, Callie. I'm not leaving you again. I made that mistake once before and it's one I won't make again."

He sounded so solemn, so sure. Callie's heart began to thrum, that same old lump lodging in her throat as she—for a second—let herself believe that he really meant it.

That he wasn't just saying what he wanted her to hear.

No. *No.* She had to protect herself. She had to protect her baby. So, rather than fall into his arms like Ash obviously expected her to, she crossed her arms over her coat and said, "I thought the fae don't make mistakes."

It was a flippant comment, but Ash surprised her by taking it seriously.

"You have a point. If it was a choice between my happiness and your life, I would've made the same choice."

"My... my life?"

Ash nodded. "Didn't you wonder why I couldn't come back? I'm fae, Callie. I live and die by the bargain.

I made a deal with Melisandre. If I stayed in Faerie, if I stayed away from you, then she'd spare your life. I accepted her terms."

It was the explanation she would've done anything to have six months ago while she was still reeling from Ash's rejection. She'd hoped it had been something like that, some noble reason why he couldn't come back to her before she remembered that he was fae. Though he'd been a different male from the one she met by the time he was gone, it was like expecting a leopard to change its spots. Fae were cunning. Callous. Demanding. They sure as hell weren't noble.

For a while there, she'd thought Ash might've been. Was she right?

Or was this just another trick?

"Then what are you doing here?" she tossed back at him.

"I told you before. I bargained for your life because it's the only one I knew about. As soon as I discovered there might be a child... I didn't bargain for anyone else. She'd kill our child, and then she'd kill you, too, just because she could. So, I figured, I'd break the bargain first. That's why I'm here. And it's why I can't go back. Even if you want to pretend our bond doesn't exist, I have a duty to my mate and my child."

"Oh, yeah?" dared Callie. "And what's that?"

"I'll stand right here, watching you. Protecting you. Whether you want me to or not. Of course, it would be easier without the door between us." Ash gestured at the apartment door. "Besides, I have even more to tell you. More to explain, if you'll let me. Maybe inside? With your permission, I should be able to step in there."

Callie thought of Mitch, still sleeping in bed. He'd be getting up soon. What was worse: her roommate meeting Ash, or Ash meeting Mitch?

"No, Ash," she said firmly. "I don't think that's a good idea."

"Because of your wards?"

She didn't ask him about how he knew she warded the apartment. He'd already confessed that something was keeping him out yesterday so she knew the warding recipe did what it was supposed to: keep faerie creatures out.

"No," she told him. "Not because of the wards."

Could she find the words? It was tough, and she struggled to tell him the rest of it—but she didn't have to. He flared his nostrils just enough, eyes narrowing when he finally figured out what she was hiding.

"The wind blew by us yesterday, bringing the scents of countless humans with it. I didn't notice... I didn't see. I do now. Better yet, I can smell it."

"Smell what?" bluffed Callie.

"Another male's scent clings to you. Not your skin... you still wear my brand so I know you haven't taken another lover. Even so, I know another male has imprinted on you." His lips thinned. "*Mitch*."

No point in denying it. Everything he said was right. She hadn't taken another lover since Ash left, but she'd only grown closer and closer to her best friend since he came back and offered to help her with her baby.

After what Ash put her through, though, she didn't owe him an explanation. With a shrug that probably wasn't as careless as she hoped, she simply said, "Yes."

The hallway felt like its temperature had gone up fifteen degrees in the next few seconds.

Callie braced herself for Ash's response. Part of her expected that Ash would, in his lord-ish manner, immediately order her to send Mitch away. That's what he had done those early days. Even before she knew he was interested in her, Ash was telling her that Mitch had to go, that he wasn't going to share her with another male, even a human one.

He'd finally stopped with that bullshit, but that was only because Mitch suddenly decided he couldn't hack living in the city anymore. She'd also figured Ash had something to do with his abrupt decision, especially since Mitch came back with his proverbial tail between his legs mere weeks after Ash chose his queen over Callie.

He had no right to be pissed that Mitch was back, Callie told herself. No right at all.

So why did the nagging feeling of guilt make her stomach queasy? Especially when Ash didn't do *anything* except funnel his anger in a way that turned the chilly corridor into a friggin' sauna.

She was just hungry, she decided. Hungry and a little bit overheated. She'd bypassed breakfast to leave the apartment before Mitch had, and now her baby was letting her know that she was hungry and uncomfortable.

"I didn't expect you were going to be out here," she said. Not a lie, since she'd been hoping to find him in the park before stumbling upon him out in the corridor. "So, if you'll excuse me, I was on my way to get breakfast."

Now that? *That* was a lie.

And Ash knew it, too.

"Callie—"

Oh, she was going to regret this. Deep down, she knew she would. But she would also regret it if she walked away from Ash and didn't resolve... this. Whatever existed between them before, and whatever they were now.

There was no changing that she was six months pregnant and that Ash was the father. Fated tied them together when Ash recognized her as his *ffrindau,* and circumstances meant that—regardless of how either of them felt—they were bonded by the child growing inside of Callie.

She took a deep breath, then sighed. "You can come with me. Okay?"

It probably wasn't what he was hoping for. She'd put money on the fact that Ash wanted her to invite him inside of her place, maybe cook for him like she had so many times before. Though he warned her never to eat food from Faerie, the fae could eat human food should they choose so long as they didn't use a metal fork. He was a huge fan of pepperoni pizza, popcorn, and scrambled eggs, she remembered, and she made plenty of brunches for the two of them to share.

That was when he was basically dating her; or the fae equivalent of dating. Now that they were going to have to co-parent for the sake of their child, he didn't get that invite or the home-cooked meal.

The deli a few blocks over would have to suffice. With a stubborn set to her jaw, she adjusted her purse hanging on the crook of her elbow and waited for his answer.

Ash gave her a solemn nod. "Of course."

WHEN CALLIE WENT to lead them inside of the deli, Ash shook his head and led her a few blocks further down until they reached a small cafe. It had small tables scattered around the space, and after Callie ordered two hot chocolates, a croissant, and a blueberry muffin, she followed Ash wordlessly toward one near the back.

It gave them privacy while also allowing Ash to keep an eye on the place. His back was to the window, his gaze roving over the handful of patrons, scrutinizing them closely. Only when he seemed to assess that the old ladies sipping their coffees and the bald man bent over his crossword weren't threats to her did he gracefully hook his fingers around the muffin, pulling toward him.

Callie was nibbling on the edge of the croissant. This close to Ash, she realized she was too nervous to really have an appetite. She picked up the nearest hot chocolate, giving Ash a quelling look when he reached for the other one.

"They're both mine," she told him.

He pulled his hand back. "Of course."

She clenched her jaw. If he said "of course" like that one more time...

This was a bad idea. When she thought she'd regret it, she figured it would be later on after Ash inevitably was gone again. Nope. The atmosphere in the cafe was *cozy* which was a nice way of saying that the tables were cramped. If she wasn't careful, she might end up brushing against him, they were seated that close.

After she took a few more tiny bites off of her

pastry, Ash plucking pieces of the muffin top and plopping it gently inside of his mouth, Callie couldn't take the tension any longer.

"Okay. Let me see if I got this straight. You tell me that you didn't want to leave me. That Melisandre made you do it. And that, all of a sudden, you could walk away from this bargain you made after all this time because you heard a rumor that a human was pregnant and you guessed it might be. Right?"

Ash nodded. "Yes. I'm glad you understand."

He was glad? She couldn't believe what she was hearing.

"So what? You could've done that all along? You just needed a reason to disobey her? Is that it?"

"Well, no. I couldn't leave until she took the cuffs off. I had to earn her trust enough that I could get to you."

Wait.

What?

"Cuffs?"

"That's right. Crystal cuffs. Magic. She could've thrown me in Siúcra—one of the prisons in Faerie," Ash added at her visibly blank look, "and I couldn't have been more trapped than I was wearing those cuffs. I only just got them off recently before I made my way back. Hearing about a possible halfling... it was the push I needed to go."

To cover up her confusion, she took a big mouthful

of her now not-so-hot chocolate, before swallowing and saying, "And you really expect me to believe all that?"

"You must." He raised his eyebrows. "Have you forgotten? I can't lie."

Callie didn't notice how hard she'd been holding onto the hope that he could, that while everything he said to her could be exaggerated, then that also meant he'd been bluffing in front of Melisandre when he said all those cold, cruel things that day in Faerie. They'd been pretty close to absolutes, and she couldn't see how she could interpret them any other way.

Guess not.

Grabbing the nearest napkin, Callie crumpled it up, tossing it on top of her picked-at food. "Really? So, then, I guess you *did* mean what you said to me before."

"Mean what? That you... that our child is in danger? I wish I wasn't."

Callie, too, but that was something she could worry about later. For now—

"'You can't forsake what you never wanted'," she retorted with more venom than she had meant to use. "I remember exactly what you said that day. And you can't lie, right?"

8

Ash's expression immediately closed off.

It just slipped out. Callie realized that she'd been holding it back since Ash suddenly reappeared in her life. Sure, she might've decided to give him a second chance rather than shut the door in his face and hide behind her wards, but it... *they...* would never work unless she got past the hurt he caused her when he rejected her in favor of the queen.

He tried to explain already. Callie hadn't been ready to listen. The way she saw it, having a fae soldier watching over her was more about the welfare of her unborn baby than it was for her sake. And maybe she'd been fooling herself that she actually *believed* that because Callie knew that she couldn't move forward until let go of the past.

She shuddered out a breath, rubbing the underside

of her belly as she met Ash's gaze. His stunning face was flat. Expressionless. It wasn't that cold, dismissive look that had twisted his handsome features, but it was just as bad.

Keeping his voice low, Ash leaned in so that only Callie could hear him. And what he said? It had shivers quivering down her spine.

"Let me make this perfectly clear. The queen demanded that I reject you. That I forsake you. To save you from her wrath, I would've done anything... you should know that, Calliope. As your bonded mate, you should believe in me. You should know there isn't a single thing I wouldn't do for you. I thought I already proved that."

Callie looked away.

Because Ash... he had. She had trusted him so implicitly that she gave him her body, her soul, and her name. That was why it hurt so fucking bad when he seemed to discard her so easily like that.

"I never lied," he continued in a voice like a lullaby. "She thought I wanted you as a toy. A pet. She neglected to understand just what you mean to me. I didn't want you. I had you, and I claimed you. I *love* you. But, more than all of that, I need you more than I've needed anything in this realm or the other."

Stay strong, Callie.

Stay strong—

She gulped. "You... you love me."

"I always have. From the moment I knew you were my *ffrindau*, you were mine. But then I got to know my white-haired beauty and there was no question. Not for me. And there shouldn't be for you, either."

"Ash—"

He cut her off with a snap of his fingers. The fire didn't catch on the first try, but when he did it again, the tiniest of flames formed at the tip of the pointer finger.

As she watched in astonishment, he created a small square. One of his fae pockets, Callie knew, and she watched as his hand disappeared into the space he made. Any one else in the cafe could've seen his trick and realized he was less than human despite his glamour, but she didn't care. Her eyes were locked on his hand as he pulled it back out of the pocket.

Between his fingers, he held the stem of a familiar yellow flower.

"Another freesia," she breathed out.

"That's right. And do you remember what it means?"

"To love someone—"

"—unconditionally," Ash finished.

Reaching out, he offered Callie his empty palm. And then her fae waited.

If she touched him, she was giving him permission. She wasn't so sure that he needed it—considering he knocked her up, she figured that was a moot point when it came to a fae and his mate—but she understood the gesture all the same.

Turning her hand over, she pressed the back of her hand against his palm.

A hint of color returned to his cheeks; instead of being sickly pale, he tanned considerably as soon as she nestled her hand in his. His eyes brightened while his lips curved in a wicked smile.

Ash pressed the freesia blooms into hers.

"I'm back," he told her. "I'm back and I'm not going anywhere. You have my heart. My loyalty. If Melisandre dared come through the portal, I'd take her head in your name. Nothing will ever separate us again... except for maybe you. Do you understand, Callie?"

She nodded, speechless.

"I can be your guard. Your soldier. I'm already your mate, but if I must prove myself again, I will. I'll do anything for you. What do you say, my *ffrindau*?"

The word was out before she even thought it.

"Okay."

It was happening again. Callie could feel herself falling harder, deeper, and she couldn't do a damn thing to stop it.

She wasn't even sure she would if she could.

She blamed her hormones. Now that she was

approaching her third trimester—and still hoping that she would have a normal pregnancy—she was consumed by them. Her estrogen levels were continuing to skyrocket, and while the pregnancy books she borrowed from the library warned her that would happen, she'd been prepared for swollen ankles, tender boobs, and such wicked heartburn, she was keeping her local pharmacy in business with all of the Tums she was buying.

An unhealthy attachment to her Light Fae? Yeah... none of her books said that might be a side effect.

It took a few days before she agreed to really give him another chance. Not as just a hired guard, but as her lover and the father of her baby. He spent every night watching over Callie as she slept, willing to stay outside of the apartment if that was the boundary she felt comfortable in enforcing. So that it was easier for Ash, she took apart more than half of her wards. She still had enough to keep a fae fresh from Faerie from getting to her, and the longer he stayed in the Iron, the easier Ash found it to put up with the salt, the iron, and the herbs.

What he *did* struggle with, though? Was knowing that, while she kept him out of her personal space, Mitch still lived in the apartment.

After their breakfast at the cafe, Ash knew better than to mention her roommate again. He seemed eager to prove that he was only looking out for Callie, and with her hitting her seventh month, he didn't want to upset her by forcing her to choose between him and Mitch.

Honestly, there was no reason for him to. By the end of that first week, Callie had fallen deep enough to realize that, if she was going to make this work, she had to do her part—and that involved sitting Mitch down one night and telling him that she was getting back with her baby's father.

He took the news well enough, his disappointment lasting for only a heartbeat before he congratulated Callie on reconciling with her ex. She could tell he was a little taken aback when she asked if it was okay that he move into her bedroom until the baby was born, but Mitch didn't even hesitate. If that's what Callie wanted, he was onboard, though he teased that he still wanted to be Uncle Mitch to the baby.

Once she got used to having Ash around again, it was like it used to be. The first time Ash got riled up over something, his aura flaring and shorting out her blender, she actually laughed. It was *exactly* like it used to be.

The only thing that really changed was how often she saw Mitch. And maybe it was because she spent most of her free time at the apartment resting in her room with Ash as company, but over the next few weeks, it seemed as if she rarely saw Mitch. She purposely did everything she could to keep the two males separated—if only because she was still worried that Ash might try to "convince" Mitch to leave again—but so long as he had her attention, Ash didn't even react like there was a third person who lived in the apartment.

Mitch did the same thing, she realized. He never even asked what her boyfriend's name was, almost as if by avoiding talking about him, he could pretend that he wasn't there. Probably not the healthiest reaction, but Callie was happy to take it if it meant they didn't argue.

Before long, Mitch started spending more and more time at the office. If he wasn't there, he was in his own room. She didn't even notice that it had been close to a week since the last time she bumped into him in the kitchen—and, considering her belly was growing by leaps and bounds lately, she meant *bump* pretty literally—until he sought her down one afternoon well into her seventh month.

She'd been laying down on the couch, her back aching, watching as Ash paced back and forth in front of her. The fae was obviously agitated, something that he didn't normally let anyone see, including Callie. Finally, when it hit the point that he couldn't stand it any longer, he told her that he needed to check something outside.

With a quick kiss to the top of her head and a

warning that she shouldn't leave the apartment, he strode toward the door.

The moment it shut behind him, the door to Mitch's room swung open.

She looked over at him, ready to say hi.

"Hey, Mitch."

"Can you talk?"

A pang of guilt stabbed her. And though she knew Ash would be back any minute now, she nodded. "Yeah. Sure."

It was her fault, after all. She hadn't meant for such a wedge to be driven between them, but it had just sort of happened. And it wasn't like she could explain to Mitch that her boyfriend was really one of the fae who was both pretty jealous and handy with a sword. Not to mention he had a way of compelling humans to do things they wouldn't usually. To keep Mitch safe, she had to keep them apart.

At least, that's what she thought... until Mitch looked around the room, seemingly searching for something. Then, when he seemed pleased that he didn't find it, he walked over to Callie.

She thought he was coming over to sit with her. Pushing herself up to her elbows, she swung her legs off of the couch, giving him room to sit next to her.

Only he didn't. Instead, grabbing her hair by the fistful, he jerked her head up where he wanted it before bending down, forcing an open-mouth kiss on an utterly shocked Callie.

It took a heartbeat for her to realize what was going on before she yanked her head out of his grip. Her lips were bruised, her head stinging from where he pulled on her hair, but she was so stinking pissed at what her roommate had just done that she barely noticed the pain.

Shoving him away from her, Callie scrambled to her feet, dashing around the back of the couch so that it was between them before she snapped at Mitch, "What the hell, dude? What were you thinking?"

Please, oh please, let him tell me that he tripped and fell and landed on my lips...

Mitch's dark eyes seemed unnaturally bright as he stalked her around the couch. There was no other word for what he was doing. He was *stalking* her like he was the predator, she was the prey, and there was nothing that was going to stop him from getting to her.

Nothing, except for a Light Fae who would come as soon as she called his name.

She opened her mouth, but Mitch managed to speak first. And what he said? Had Callie stunned into silence.

"I couldn't take it any longer. Knowing another man is with you. Touching you. Kissing you. That should be me."

Her eyes went wide.

He didn't just say...

"I'm supposed to be the dad. Not him. Not the deadbeat. *Me*. It was always meant to be me. I can't keep it to myself anymore—"

Finally understanding that he was getting way, way too close, Callie threw up her hands, trying her best to ward him off. "You really should, Mitch. I mean... we're friends. That's all. You *know* that."

"No. I know that I'm in love with you. I've always been in love with you."

"This is crazy—"

"I've always been in love with you."

"*You*'re crazy."

Mitch's lips split in a wide grin that she'd never seen him wear before. "Maybe so, but I'm crazy in love with you. This is me, finally taking my shot."

She shook her head, her white-blonde hair whipping her in her face with how fast she moved. "You really don't want to do this, Mitch."

"Run away with me, Callie," he pleaded, backing her toward the kitchen. "Be mine. We can leave right now and that fae of yours will never, ever know. Trust me."

Callie froze.

Trust him?

Trust him?

When he knew that Ash was a fae and he was only just telling her that?

HIS SENSES WERE DULLED, but he was still an elite soldier. Over the iron and the noise, the stink of human waste, Ash caught a hint of Faerie lingering too close to Callie's home.

In the few weeks since he'd been living near, then with Callie—staying in her bedroom with her while she was home, following her down to the portrait stop when she insisted on going to her workplace—he'd sensed it a few times, but nothing as strong at what was hitting him now.

It had been irking him since early that morning. He thought it would be a fluke. With Callie's wards, very few of the faerie folk came near the apartment, but some passed by near enough for him to sense them. Assuming it was as simple as that, he ignored it.

Hours later, though, and it hadn't dimmed. It hadn't grown stronger, either, and that concerned him. Unless he was wrong, and he doubted he was, it seemed as if someone was keeping watch outside. Just like how he used to stand at his post for hours at a time under Melisandre's orders, it was like the presence he sensed was unmoving.

When he finally couldn't stand it any longer, he told Callie he was going to go check. He only planned on taking the ten flights of stairs to the ground floor, then doing a circle around her block.

Turns out, that wasn't necessary. The moment he stepped out of the lobby, he felt the pull of Faerie like an undeniable beacon. Narrowing his gaze on the street in front of him, he searched for the source, but didn't see anything. Jogging closer, he followed the pull toward the ground where he found an apple.

Ash bent down, grabbing it. Beneath his glamour, his eyes sparked in recognition when he saw that the half-eaten apple wasn't just *any* apple. It was more pink than red, with a crystalline sheen, and a sugary taste he knew very well.

It was a Faerie apple, taken straight from the Fae Queen's garden.

Ash squeezed the fruit, pulp spraying to the ground and the stick juice ran down his wrist.

Melisandre.

9

Ash spun on his heel when he heard someone approaching. Only centuries worth of a soldier's reflexes kept him from slamming into the little human female with her even smaller creature.

No. Not creature, he remembered. What had Callie told him it was called? Ah, yes. The little human female and her smaller dog.

The human had hair even whiter than Callie's. Her wrinkly skin showed her age, though she was far younger than one of his kind. As she led her dog on a leash, her back was stopped, a slight frown on her face as she wagged a finger at the pulverized apple in his grip.

"Kids these days. Throwing a perfectly good apple

on the ground after a few bites when there's a garbage right there."

So there was.

Before she realized that he'd smashed it with his hand, Ash walked over to the trash can, dropping the mangled ruins of the apple into the bin.

Turning back, he saw that she was watching him now. Though all of the humans seemed to look the same to Ash, he thought this one looked familiar. The creature certainly did.

And then she said, "I know you. You're the one who's just moved in with the pretty pregnant girl and her Mitch, aren't you?"

The glamour showed the woman a friendly human face, though the fae scowled to hear her so easily refer to Mitch as Callie's even as he said, "That's me, yes."

"Will you be leaving, too?"

"Excuse me?"

"That's what Mitch told me. That they're leaving at the end of the month. Moving out. Shame, though. Such a handsome family. I would've liked to have met the baby, but I understand. He wants what's best for his wife."

Ash nearly dropped his glamour.

It was one thing for this human neighbor to think of Mitch that way, as Callie's. For better or worse, he couldn't keep her from her friend unless he wanted to risk pushing her away again.

But Callie wasn't Mitch's wife.

She was *his* mate.

And leaving? She wasn't going anywhere without him.

Though it was clear that the human female wanted to talk more, Ash had already been out of the building for longer than he wanted to. Especially now that he wanted to find out if there was any truth in what the female told him, he quickly made his excuses before striding toward the stairs again.

And if he wasn't as pleasant as Callie would've liked him to be, oh well.

Because Callie still guessed that Ash had compelled Mitch to leave last summer—which, of course, he *had*—he'd made a point not to force the topic of her roommate moving out again. Once the baby came, he'd find a way to explain to Callie that keeping Mitch around was only adding him to the danger, but he was doing everything he could to keep his mate happy with him.

When she finally let Ash come into the apartment to stay, the only thing she asked of him was to leave Mitch alone. So he had.

Now, humans have scents. Ash usually ignored them since most made his skin crawl. Since living in the Iron, he'd grown accustomed to muting most of his senses so that he didn't waste any of his lingering power. He knew Callie's instinctively, the way everything about her was imprinted on every inch of him; nothing else mattered. But when Ash walked into the apartment, following his pull toward Callie to the kitchen, he paused.

With the human male looming over his mate while Callie exuded a combination of anger and fear, he couldn't stop himself from opening up to her roommate.

He'd thought it was strange that, while Callie was careful to keep the two males apart, her roommate didn't argue. He stayed out of sight of Ash, keeping to himself in his room when he was home. Since Ash didn't want to face the other male, he was glad even if he thought it odd.

But now Ash knew why Mitch stayed human—because he wasn't just a human.

He was touched by a fae.

And the brand on his skin? Ash was very familiar with it.

One look in the human's crazed dark eyes and he knew. Add that to the whirl of fae magic cloaking him and the apple he found planted outside—right where he could easily leave it—and Ash was positive.

"Callie. Come to me."

She spun at the sound of his voice, relief washing over her. "Ash. Thank God you're here. Now, I don't know what you think is going on here, but Mitch was just leaving."

"Calliope." As her bonded mate, he couldn't compel her with her true name, but he poured as much urgency into those four syllables as he could. "To me. Now."

Unaware of how much danger she was currently in, she held up her finger—a human signal for him to wait —before she glanced over at the touched human again.

"Right, Mitch?" she said again.

"Callie!"

She jolted at his shout, turning back to look at him again. "What?"

"That's not Mitch."

WHAT?

So consumed with watching Ash, of trying to make sense of the insane thing he just said, she didn't realize that her roommate had lashed out a hand, grabbing her around her upper arm, until her whole body rocked.

Callie gasped, her balance thrown.

Forever fast, Ash lunged for her. While Mitch tried to yank her toward him again, Ash did everything he could to steady her, to keep her from falling.

She stumbled, finally finding her feet as she panted heavily. Her heart was beating like a drum as she thought about how close she came to tumbling right over. What if she had fallen? Landed on her baby?

Frantic fear at the what-if's made her angry. Once Ash took control, leading her away from an oddly smirking Mitch, she spun on him ready to let him have it. First the kiss, now this? What the hell was going on with him?

"Callie, no—"

Ash lunged for her again, grabbing her by both upper arms, dragging her against his chest just in time for her to miss the flat of the palm that had been streaking straight for her cheek.

Her jaw dropped as it dawned on her what had just happened.

Mitch had just tried to slap her!

Okay. Something really wrong was going on now, she thought wildly, leaning back into Ash. Her fae squeezed her arms gently before quickly maneuvering her behind him.

Mitch made a move to follow but, before he had taken a single step, Ash held up his hand.

Standing partly behind him, partly next to him, Callie watched as his eyes swirled, a menacing display of molten lava rolling over the gold.

"Stay, pet."

Mitch went statue-still.

Literally.

He didn't move. Didn't even friggin' breathe either. Even his eyes stopped moving without a single blink.

She tugged on Ash's sleeve. "What's going on here? Ash? Tell me!"

Reaching behind him, never taking his gaze off of Mitch, he patted her thigh. "Stay here. Don't move. And don't let him touch you."

Before she could say another word, Ash surged forward. He held out his hand. "Give me yours," he ordered. "Let me touch you."

"Ash," she hissed.

He ignored her as the Mitch statue jerkily picked up his hand before dropping it into Ash's outstretched palm. A quick touch and then Ash dropped it.

"You wear my brand now," he told Mitch. "You will answer me."

"Yes."

Callie gasped. Because that voice? It came out of Mitch, but it sure as hell wasn't his.

That's not Mitch...

Then who was it?

Ash seemed to be thinking along the same lines as Callie. "Who are you?"

"I... I don't know."

"Fair enough. Do you know who owns you?"

"Yes."

"Who?"

"Melisandre."

"By touch?"

"Mitch" shook his head, pained. "Faerie fruit. She gave me an apple and now I'm a—"

"Slave."

"Yes."

Ash's expression went chiseled, like he was carved from stone. "You'll never be free."

"She promised me freedom if I gained the trust of the human mate and brought her the halfling child. I set out a lure to get the fae out of the apartment and I made my move. By tonight, I would've been free."

And the fae can't lie.

Ash hefted his sword. "There's only one way you'll be free. Whether by one of her soldier's blades or by mine, death comes for you."

Callie gasped again.

But the man didn't react the same way. In fact, she swore he looked almost... relieved as he said in Mitch's voice, "I know."

She was watching the fake Mitch now, searching for some clue that it wasn't her roommate but, in fact, one of Melisandre's humans. There was nothing. He looked exactly like Mitch, and though Callie's sight wasn't exactly foolproof, she was positive that this man wasn't wearing any glamour.

But it wasn't Mitch. It couldn't be.

And she was still thinking that when, out of the corner of her eye, she saw Ash move.

Where had he pulled the gleaming, glittering diamond-edged sword from? She had no idea, but the instant she saw it, she knew exactly what he was going to do with it it. And, with one perfectly positioned thrust, he did.

Just like how he ran that kobold throw on the tip of his sword, he plunged it right through the center of her roommate's chest.

"Ash! No!"

"It had to be this way," her fae said softly, pulling the sword back out of the fake Mitch's chest. "He knew it, too. There was nothing else to be done."

She didn't want to believe it. She started to argue, but stopped when she saw that the stabbed man had crumpled to the kitchen floor.

Immediately, she knew he was dying, if not already dead.

And she knew that Ash was right. That *wasn't* Mitch.

Right in front of her eyes, he began to change. The blond hair darkened. The handsome face turned rounder, fuller, as the nose grew a little longer. He had a shadow of a goatee around his jaw, and blank black eyes staring up at the ceiling.

Around his neck, he wore a gold chain that Callie had never noticed on Mitch before. Following the length of it, she saw that it ended with a hunk of pale pink crystal that nestled in the hollow of his throat.

She couldn't bring herself to look any further south. As Ash moved his blade out of her line of vision, she purposely kept her eyes on his throat before pointing a shaky finger at the crystal.

"What is that?"

More to himself than Callie, Ash said, "It's not a Brinkburn."

"A what?"

"Fae killer."

Callie's hand shot to her belly as her voice a couple of octaves. "*What*?"

Ash dropped his bloody sword as he hurriedly backed away from the body, turning to Callie. Careful of her bump, he pulled her into his embrace, ducking her head against his shoulder as he whispered soothingly, "It's not. I would've known... it's okay. That crystal can't hurt us."

But it wasn't okay. Mitch was dead, only that wasn't Mitch. But the fake Mitch confessed that the real Mitch was gone and—

"Breathe, my mate. You have to breathe. Look." Steadying her with one hand, he stepped away from her, dropping to one knee. He wrapped the chain around his fist, yanking it from the dead man with a sharp tug. Lifting it up, he showed it to Callie. "It's just a crystal. Fae magic."

She took a few deep breaths, desperate to calm

herself. When she thought she had, she focused on the shimmering pink crystal.

"Wait. That... that's why I didn't know? Why I couldn't see through him and tell he was a fake? That crystal made him look like Mitch?"

Ash nodded. "If they imprinted it right, it would've given him your Mitch's memories, too. He would've been able to fool everyone, even those closest to him."

Like her. Like his family. His employers, too.

She'd never doubted for a moment that the man she lived with was the Mitch she'd known for years. Apart from his weird fixation with fruit—which was readily explained now that she knew he was addicted to faerie fruit—he'd been exactly the same guy until the moment he forced himself on her like that.

Callie was glad that Ash killed the fake Mitch. He deserved it. But though the panic she felt when she first thought that *her* Mitch was dead wasn't as uncontrollable as it was only a few moments ago, she had to ask.

She had to *know*.

"But if he was pretending to be Mitch to... to..." Callie gulped, unable to even say it. She tamped down the rising panic, doing her best to spit her question out. "If that's not Mitch, then where is he? Where's my old roommate, Ash?"

"It's possible that—"

"No." *It's possible that...* a phrase like that was how the fae got around telling the truth. In her state, she needed honesty, not platitudes. "I don't want to know what's possible. You told me that she would do anything to stop me from having my baby. You know her. You know what she would do. What happened to Mitch?"

Ash must've heard something in her tone that had him realizing that she was serious.

Taking her hand, giving her fingers a squeeze, he said flatly, "She would've had him killed so that her pet could take his place. To make the crystal to do what it had to, the mortal would've been sacrificed."

Her voice dropped to a whisper as her chest felt like it was being squeezed. *No.* "Are you sure?"

"I'm sorry, my mate, but you met Melisandre. What do you think?"

Her fae had a very valid point.

Which meant that Mitch was very dead.

A sob rose up in her throat as she jerked her hand out of his hold. She wasn't sure if it was for Mitch, or for herself. For the sudden way she had to learn that he was gone, that he was replaced by someone for Faerie, or how the fake Mitch had been lying in wait, his orders to get his hands on Callie's baby no matter what he had to do.

For weeks, Ash impressed upon her how much danger she was in. Melisandre would stop at nothing to get at their child, and she thought she understood that.

Had she?

Staring down at the unfamiliar face, careful not to look any lower at the fatal wound in his chest, she had to admit that she might've downplayed the threat.

Bile took the place of the sob. She was shaking, her head spinning. The edge of her vision went dark as her legs went weak. Recognizing the signs, she backed up before turning, sprinting toward the bathroom.

Her fae had missed the early months. He hadn't seen the way she suffered from morning sickness. When she bolted, he must have assumed the worse, immediately chasing after her.

For once, though, she was quicker.

Callie slammed the door in Ash's face, throwing the lock a split second before she dropped to her knees, emptying the contents of her stomach into the toilet with a sickening splash.

She threw up two more times until there was nothing left. Shaky from heaving, she braced her arms on the toilet seat. Her mouth tasted nasty, her eyes burned, but she stayed where she was, wincing when the knock started.

"Callie? Callie... tell me you're okay."

Ash.

She swallowed, wincing as the acrid taste of vomit hit the back of her throat. Waiting until she could speak without moaning, she said, "I'm not, but I will be."

Probably wasn't the right thing to say. Ash's answer had a touch of panic that was strange and new as he said, "Let me in."

"Uh-uh."

"Then come back out here." Ash paused for a moment, before saying, "Please."

If she hadn't just discovered that she'd been living with a stranger these last few months, hearing Ash say 'please' might've been Callie's biggest shock of the afternoon.

"I will. Just... just give me a minute. Can I have a minute?"

Through the wood, she heard Ash's sighed, followed by his musical voice murmur, "You can have everything you want."

If only she could believe that.

10

Ash's first instinct was to grab Callie and pull her close. Though time ran differently between realms, he knew it had been six months in the human world that she'd been on her own—and it seemed to drag even longer while he was in Faerie while he was forcefully separated from her. Now that he was with her again, it... it *pained* him to have her put any space between them now that she'd relented and let him back into her home.

And if there was one thing a powerful fae loathed, it was pain.

He wanted her. He wanted to hold her, to comfort her, to draw strength from her touch. The bathroom wasn't warded. Weakened as he was, he could still break in there if he had to. But he wouldn't. If Callie needed a few moments alone to process everything, Ash would give them to her.

He'd give her the world if she asked for it.

For the moment, he settled on taking care of the dead body instead.

Ash knew Callie. Knew that she was too soft, too young, too *good* to understand that death was sometimes unavoidable. With his tie to the Fae Queen, the pet was already as good as dead from the moment he first fell for Melisandre's charm. Ash had seen it happen countless time over the years. She would find a pet, trick them into faerie food so that they had to rely on her, then grow bored. Some of her humans ended up in her garden, some were gifted to her nobles, and many starved to death when she stopped feeding them.

It was a well-known fae tactic. Give a human faerie food—specifically its charmed fruit—and they could eat nothing but that. If it didn't carry the touch of Faerie on it, the food turned to ash in their mouths. They couldn't swallow, and most stopped trying. The most common way a slave to the fruit perished was starvation long after their fae master or mistress simply forgot about them.

The human was dead from the moment he trusted Melisandre's glamour, believing that the lovely Fae Queen was benevolent and innocent rather than cunning and cruel. He had a reprieve while she kept him frozen a statue in her garden, but his fate was sealed once she sent him into the Iron.

Food would run out. He would fail and she would have him executed. Or, as unlikely as it might've seemed, Callie could have figured out the truth.

She hadn't—but Ash had.

He was a dead man walking all along, but the second Ash saw the betrayal flash across his mate's face to realize she'd been tricked, nothing could have stopped him from running his sword through the queen's touched human.

He'd seen that look once before. When he rejected Callie for her own sake, doing the same thing that the human had done: following Melisandre's orders. He vowed that, if he found his way back to Callie, he'd never stand by and watch her face fall like that again.

And he didn't.

The human was dead. Melisandre would figure that out sooner than later, but they had some time. Not much. It was dark out now, the time of shadows, so the queen—clinging to her facade that she was a Light Fae—wouldn't react until at least morning in the Iron. Still, they had to be far away from this place by then.

He couldn't leave the body behind when they fled. Ash had no idea how long this mortal had been controlled by his queen. Years? Decades? Longer? He didn't have Mitch's face any longer, but there would still be questions if the human authorities discovered a corpse in Callie's home.

When Ash was in full control of his powers, disposing of the touched human's remains would be simple enough. With a palm full of faerie fire, he could conjure a large pocket that connected him to the other side of the veil. The most he could call to him was a pinch that opened a fist-sized gap. Enough for him to draw his sword out of, but not to vanish a human.

His sun-colored gaze darted to the closed bathroom door. So long as Callie was safe behind there, he was willing to strike a deal.

Reaching into his pocket, Ash felt the familiar curve of the small pebble, squeezing it before tucking it deeper. His request wasn't worth the life debt, not yet, but it was reassuring nonetheless that he still held control over Nine's geas.

One day, he would probably need it. Until then, he would rely on what he had to work with, and if there was one thing he'd learned during his days at the Shadow Academy, it was just how hungry those shadows were.

Keeping his voice low, careful not to disturb his grieving mate, Ash called out, "Ninetroir. I command you to appear."

If it was during the sunlight, Ash would only be able to summon the Dark Fae if he was standing near a patch of enchanted shadow so black, it was like a piece of night seeping out in the day. Luckily, it was already night, and he knew in an instant that Nine was curious enough to answer his command.

There were only two of Callie's warding packets left in the apartment; she'd removed most of them when Ash came to stay with her. It was a slight warning to a faerie creature rather than a barrier, and it didn't deter Nine from slowly materializing right next to him.

He was frowning, black curls wafting in the breeze of his shadows as they carried him from Faerie to the Iron. Already so pale, Ash couldn't tell if the wards affected the Dark Fae, though the way his nose wrinkled made him think it did.

And then in the harsh voice so undeniably Nine, he said, "It reeks of humans and death in here, Aislinn. Where in Oberon's name have you brought me?"

Ash wasn't surprised to hear Nine invoke the missing Summer King's name. He knew that Nine had no love lost for Melisandre, though he would've thought Nine would call on Morrigan instead. He was a Dark Fae, after all, and she was the lost Winter Queen.

Hmm...

With a rough shake that had his long, tawny hair spilling over one shoulder, he pushed those thoughts aside. What did it matter who Nine gave his loyalty to? It obviously wasn't Melisandre, and that was the only reason why Ash lowered himself enough to summon Nine with his true name.

"The human realm."

"I had hoped I was mistaken, but I wasn't. The iron is especially strong here."

"It's not just the iron," Ash confessed. "My mate is resourceful. She has iron mixed with salt and herbs warding her home."

"Your mate. The human female?"

Ash nodded.

Nine's eyes were silver, the color and sheen of a polished mirror, and they brightened notably when he realized exactly where in the Iron he was. "Where is she? I want to meet the human who was worth a soldier of the Court betraying his queen."

He supposed he deserved that jab. After all, that was exactly what Ash had done. He'd do it again, too, given the chance. Duty to his mate, to his *ffrindau*, was the only thing that trumped his duty to the Fae Queen. One day when Nine found his, he'd understand.

"Occupied," he said, his clipped tone warning Nine to drop it. If he had his way, none of his kind would ever meet his mate again. "That's not why I summoned you."

With a slight nod, Nine conceded that point. "So why did you?"

The fae guarded their names fiercely. Countless souls

knew that Ash's true name was Aislinn, but unless he gave that name to them, they couldn't use it against him. After Ash saved Nine, Nine tried to trade his name for the pebble. Tricky as ever, Ash took the name as a gift rather than a bargain, retaining his hold on Nine's life debt.

Just because he could summon Nine, though, that didn't mean that he would. This was the first time that he had, which proved that while the Dark Fae had been forced to visit the Iron, he still had all of the control in this situation.

"You scented death. You're right." With a wave of his hand, Ash drew Nine's attention toward the fallen human, sprawled out and bleeding on Callie's kitchen floor. "You're right."

Striding silently, his shadowy cloak traveling behind him, he moved past Ash. A slight twitch of his perfect features as he spied the human before he admitted, "I've seen him before."

"He was one of Melisandre's humans."

Nine scoffed. "Humans."

Ash chose to ignore that. Like most of his kind— like Ash, once upon a time—Nine's disdain for humans was legendary. He thought of them as little more than goblins, only far more breakable. He couldn't understand why one of the fae would want anything to do with the Iron. Touching a human? *Mating* a human? He couldn't hide his hated for them, but that was just fine. Their shared hatred of Melisandre was enough for Ash to look past it.

"I had to kill him. She sent him after mine." He waited for a moment that seemed like an eternity before he admitted, "And my child."

His gaze slid over to Ash. "Ah. So the rumors *are* true."

Ash didn't answer. His silence was enough for Nine.

"Very well. Still, that doesn't answer my question, Aislinn. Why have you called *me*?"

The Dark Fae knew. Even if he hadn't sensed death as he was summoned to the Iron, once he spied the human sprawled out on Callie's floor, Nine would've known why Ash used his true name the way he had.

Of course, he wouldn't admit that. Just like he would never offer any help. It wasn't how the fae did things, and even if Ash lost most of his tie to Faerie since he chose to stay in the Iron with his human mate, he was still fae.

"To propose a deal."

Cocking his head slightly, Nine's silver eyes gleamed. "I'm listening."

"Take the human."

"Why?"

Normally, Ash would never answer to another fae. To do so was acknowledging that they had a right to question you, and Nine was both a younger fae *and*

Unseelie. In Faerie, Ash was also much higher in the ranks than Nine was. Ash owed him nothing.

Normally.

But things weren't normal. They hadn't been since Melisandre posted him along the veil in an act of petty revenge and Ash stumbled upon a white-haired beauty with the sight.

So, swallowing his pride, he explained to Nine just what was asking for.

"Melisandre charmed one of her human's to look like a friend of my mate's. When I realized the deception, I killed him, but my mate is soft-hearted. It pains her to see the remains even though she knows he never really was her friend. If it pains her, it pains me. I want him gone. I want you to take him."

"Oh?" Nine's tongue darted out, licking the corner of his mouth. "Why do you think I would do that? For the pebble?"

Nice try, Nine, thought Ash.

"No. This is a different bargain. I give you the human, you give it to the shadows. That's the deal I'm offering you."

A hint of disappointment flashed across Nine's face, there and gone again. It didn't linger only because Ash was crafty. It wasn't a life debt, but the bargain was still a good one—and they both knew it.

A touch was full of pleasure and power; it came from the piece of a mortal soul that the fae can siphon with the brush of their fingers. When it came to the Dark Fae, though, their magic was rooted in the shadows. Especially for one like Nine, who could gather shadows to him, weaving them to make the shadowy cloak he wore or creating portals of his own that he could shade-walk through, it was the source of his powers.

The shadows were often hungry. If he fed the human's remains to the shadows, it would be out of Callie's sight, out of Melisandre's reach, and a boost to Nine's strength.

A perfect bargain without Ash having to resort to burning Nine's life debt.

Nine stayed quiet for a few moments. He was as still as the grave, his dark curls still billowing softly, the tail of his cloak floating behind him. Though the Dark Fae was firmly on this side of the veil, his shadow magic kept him covered in Faerie magic. The iron in the apartment was probably draining it faster than Nine would ever allow Ash to guess, but he was still strong enough to put on a display for the Light Fae.

Finally, as Ash waited on bated breath, Nine nodded. "Deal."

Bending one knee, he laid his palm against the dead human's cheek. The air grew heavy, a chilly wind whistling down the hall, and when Ash couldn't keep himself from spinning to make sure that Nine hadn't summoned wind spirits to Callie's home, he missed whatever it was that Nine did to the dead human.

Only a few seconds had passed when he spun back to find that Nine was standing again. The kitchen floor was completely empty. There wasn't a single drop of spilled blood to mark where the human had fallen. It was almost as if he have never died there at all.

The shadows took it all. One look at Nine—whose pale skin was glowing like the moon, his silver eyes swirling with a madness Ash had seen there once or twice before—and Ash knew that this bargain had been heavily weighted in Nine's favor.

Good. The pebble was still tucked securely in his pocket where it belonged.

At least, that's what Ash thought—until Nine's expression turned as dark as his shadows.

"Our deal is done. The shadows have feasted. But Aislinn... you dared to use my name while weak from iron. Only knowing I owe you a geas kept me from taking advantage of that. Do you understand?"

"Ninetroir—"

The rush of Unseelie magic pouring off of Nine had Ash stumbling. Pride kept him standing, but it wasn't easy.

He nodded. Warning understood.

Nine pointed one long, slender, white finger at Ash. "The next time you dare summon me, be prepared to trade back that damned pebble—or don't summon me at all."

With that, Nine blinked out, leaving darkness and a chill in his wake.

Yes. Definitely understood.

HE WARNED HER. He warned her that choosing him was dangerous, that the queen would stop at nothing to get to their baby.

She just never expected that included killing her friend and using crystal magic from Faerie to transfigure one of her touched mortals to take his place for *months*.

When did the switch take place? Was the man who came back in early September, begging her for forgiveness and hoping she'd let him return to the apartment the real Mitch? Or was he already gone?

How could she tell his parents when she didn't really understand it all herself? And how could she confess that, whatever happened, she was the reason why their son was dead?

She couldn't. She wasn't strong enough. Just like she wasn't strong enough to face Ash yet.

She lost track of how long she hid in the bathroom. At one point, she swore she heard voices, but since no one came to the door, she fell back on her old standby: she pretended that she didn't.

Too bad she couldn't pretend forever.

It wasn't fair, leaving Ash out there with the fake Mitch. It was hard for her to face the truth, but hiding from it didn't make it go away. She was made of stronger stuff than that and, after a while, she pushed up from the toilet seat where she'd been perched before reaching for the doorknob.

Pushing open the door, she found Ash standing opposite of her, as if he'd been waiting for her to come to him again.

He'd been standing at attention, the perfect soldier, but he went even stiffer when he saw the door open.

"Callie."

Her voice broke as she whispered his name.

It was strangely cold in the hall, she noticed. Dark, too, as if more of the lights had blown.

And, maybe she was being a bit dramatic, but it seemed as still as the grave...

She hesitated. She didn't want to move too far from the bathroom just yet in case she got close enough to the kitchen and she saw the body again. That didn't stop her gaze from drifting in that direction, though. Even when Ash quickly assured her that it was gone, that he'd taken care of it for her, she stayed in the doorway, leaning against the jamb.

Her legs were shaky, her hands protecting the swell

of her belly. She choked back a sob as she met Ash's gaze again.

In the next breath, he'd closed the gap between them. He pulled her into his loving embrace, careful not to squeeze even as she felt his warmth envelope her.

Collapsing against him, Ash took her weight, supporting her as he whispered heated promises in her ear.

It's going to be okay.

I won't let anyone hurt you.

I'm with you.

I'll protect you.

You're mine—

The fae can't lie, she told herself as she clung to her mate. And though it seemed as if her world had turned upside-down again for the third time in less than a year, at least she still had Ash.

—and I love you.

11

Though he was much stronger than a mortal, Ash didn't have enough power to create a Light Fae portal. He tried—burning through the last of his reserves, he tried—but the most he conjured were a few sparks between his forefinger and his thumb.

That was a huge problem. Now that Melisandre's pet had been compromised, it wouldn't be long before she sent someone else to check on Callie, especially now that the dead human's plan to bring Callie before the Fae Queen had failed. They had to leave, but traveling through a portal was out of the question.

Nibbling on her nail, Callie suggested in a blank voice that they could turn to her family for help. Ash had to gently point out why that wasn't a good idea. To get at their child, Melisandre wouldn't think twice about ordering the deaths of a few more humans.

She couldn't help but keep looking down at the blank space where the human had died. She finally accepted that that wasn't her friend, but that didn't change the fact that the Mitch she knew was also gone. If she ran to her hometown, she was putting her family at risk.

And Callie would never do that.

Between Callie and Mitch, they shared one car. Living in the city, relying on public transportation made more sense than maintaining a vehicle and paying for a parking space. Technically, it belonged to Mitch, and he'd driven it home when he left last summer. Whoever it was that returned it—real Mitch or fake Mitch—Callie knew that the car was nearby.

It was something at least.

Ash didn't argue when she suggested it. She could tell he wasn't a fan of the idea. In Faerie, the fae relied on a horse and carriage if they couldn't use their portals, and he'd never ridden in a car before.

First time for everything, right?

Callie grasped at the whisper of a plan with both hands, holding tight. Plotting their next step gave her something to focus on that wasn't poor Mitch's fate and how she'd spent months living with a stranger—

"Mitch always kept the keys in his room, I'm betting the fake Mitch did, too," she told Ash, speaking louder than normal as if to drown out her intrusive thoughts. "I'll go get them."

"Let me."

She shook her head. It would be too easy to let Ash take over for her, but she had something just as important to stand up for. Melisandre fucked up by targeting her baby. So what if she couldn't take on the queen herself? Or that she'd been fooled by the fake Mitch? She still had her sight, and she was going to use it.

The time for pretending was over. Callie was going to take every advantage that she had to stay one step ahead of her.

"I got it. But give me a sec, then we can start packing up whatever we need to get the hell out of here."

There was no time to make proper arrangements. She hated that she was running out without letting Buster now, and she hoped her landlord didn't flip out when she broke her lease.

What else could she do? Stick around and wait for the queen to try again?

No fucking way.

Setting her expression in a look of grim determination, she cupped the edge of Ash's jaw, giving him a jolt of power with her touch. Some of his color returned, and though he leaned into her palm, nuzzling her with his cheek, he stayed quiet when Callie shuffled past him, heading for Mitch's room.

The keys were tossed on top of his dresser. So was his wallet.

Callie quickly pocketed the keys, her hand hovering over the wallet as she grabbed for that next. Melisandre's seemingly innocent smile flashed before her mind's eye, firming her resolve. Mitch was dead, she reminded herself. What use did he have for money now?

She snagged the wallet, shoving it in her back pocket.

After that, it was a blur. She'd always known that Ash was a soldier first, a guard second, and he proved it. Fae or not, when Callie barked orders at her mate, he immediately jumped into action.

Less than an hour later, she'd packed every piece of luggage and storage case she owned with whatever she couldn't replace. Ash used glamour to shield them as he made three trips up and down the ten flights, packing the car for her. Since the last thing she wanted was for one of her neighbors to figure out she was moving out, when she left her apartment for the last time, the only thing Callie carried was her prized camera and the bag full of lenses.

Just a regular day, she thought. A regular day when she went out to shoot the local scenery.

And, no, she wasn't running for her life... why do you ask?

Ash was already sitting inside of the car when she

anxiously met him in the parking garage. Callie passed him her camera bag as she dropped onto the driver's seat, purposely choosing not to notice how much paler he seemed. The car wasn't doing him any favors. The iron in the steel frame was too much, but what else could they do? Especially since the queen would never expect Ash would sicken himself by willingly riding inside of the car—which was precisely why he told her drive when Callie hesitated behind the wheel.

The iron might make him sick, but if the queen found them, that would be the least of their worries.

Helix knew where to find Callie. As soon as Melisandre learned that her human pet was killed, she would send someone else to the apartment. They had to get as far away as possible.

She didn't have a destination in mind when she peeled out of the lot; her intention was to get out of the city and as far away from the suburbs where her family lived. Ash suggested another big city full of iron since, in the human realm, his kind were drawn to the few patches of nature and greenery that remained. Melisandre's soldiers would follow them everywhere, but finding a tall building surrounded by iron that she could cover in her wards... if they were lucky, it should buy them some time until their child was born, at least.

Three hours later and close to two hundred miles away from her apartment, Mitch's car started to shudder. Callie wasn't sure if it was because she was pushing it harder than she should have, but a few minutes later, the front headlight popped.

Ash cursed under his breath.

She dug her fingers into the backside of the steering wheel.

His power might have faded, but Ash was still fae. He was still inherently magic. Considering how many appliances, lights, and tech his presence in her apartment had blown out since she'd known him, she probably should've expected that he would do something to a friggin' *car*.

"I'm going to take the next exit," she said, raising her voice over the whine coming from the front of the car. The engine? Probably. "We don't want to be walking on the highway if we can help it."

"We need to get somewhere high," was all Ash said.

A hotel, Callie figured. Until they could find somewhere else to hide out, something more permanent, she would have to find them a hotel that was taller than a few stories. If Ash wanted them off the ground, she wasn't going to argue.

For once that night, luck was finally on her side. When the car finally gave out—and it did, jolting to a stop as the engine dropped with a *thunk*—it died on the outskirts of Newport, one of the biggest cities the next state over.

Or, as Callie would come to think of it, her new home.

To Ash, the apartment they rented, then warded on the fourteenth floor was just the same as the one Callie used to live in. It was essentially an iron cage, and only his determination to keep his mate and child safe had him willingly locking himself inside of it.

Living with the wards was hard. It was like sludging through tar those first few days after she set pouches around the space, but he put up with it because he knew it would be close to impossible for someone with faerie blood to get past them. The more he grew accustomed to them—grew accustomed to the human world—the easier he found it to tolerate them.

But if Ash could tolerate them, then so could one of the fae. He pushed Callie to add more wards, only putting a limit when she confessed that she was worried about him. About how he was visibly affected by the countless sachets littered around their home.

It was, admittedly, a bit of a shock to him. He'd never had another soul be concerned for him; before Callie, he'd never shown concern for another soul, either. He was more than willing to risk his own life to save hers, but he couldn't bear to see her be worried for him.

Ever since he claimed her, everything he did was in the name of his *ffrindau*. He didn't just have to save her from Melisandre. In a way, he needed to save her from himself.

And he did. Whatever she wanted, he gave it to her. When she was worried that money was running out, he found some. He was fae, not mortal. It didn't matter that he was living in the human world now. He wasn't human, would never be human, and he didn't think like a human.

Callie wanted money. He got it for her.

She wanted a roof over her head. Done.

She wanted to protect their child with a fierceness only a mother would? He might not be able to conjure enough faerie fire to open a portal, but he still was connected to his pocket in Faerie. As he proved when he killed Melisandre's pet, he had his sword at hand whenever he needed it.

He'd wielded that diamond-edged blade for centaurs, always in the queen's honor. It was his duty.

For Callie, he'd turn that sword on anyone if only she asked him to.

She owned him. From that first touch, he'd been hers. She might have offered him a piece of her soul, but his heart—icy cold until she thawed it out for him —belonged to Callie.

And it always would.

DESPITE HOW HE did everything he could to make the last few months of Callie's pregnancy as calm and as easy as possible, it wasn't really a surprise when the baby came a few weeks earlier than they'd been hoping it would.

Still, they were prepared. One room of their apartment had been turned into a nursery specifically for their child. Because they agreed that they couldn't risk going to a human hospital just in case, Callie had used the Yellow Pages to find a practicing midwife in Newport when she was eight months along.

Even after living in the Iron for two months, he still retained two of his powers: the ability to cloak himself in glamour and how easily he could compel weak-minded humans to do what he wanted, touch or no touch. He charmed the midwife, a fifty-something human woman called Louise, implanting the suggestion that, when Callie called for her, she would drop everything and come to the apartment.

It was a short labor, though that might've been because neither Ash nor Callie recognized that the slight twinges she felt were actually contractions up until the moment her water broke. She made the call, Louise arrived within fifteen minutes, and Ash was shooed out of the bedroom where Callie was laid up.

Wracked with worry for his growing family, Ash's aura flared. For the first time in weeks, his fae power surged enough to have three separate bulbs popping, leaving the glass shards to twinkle against the tile.

He couldn't risk exploding another. Or, worse, the reach of his aura burning out the light in the bedroom while Callie was giving birth.

Instead, he busied himself with cleaning up the mess so that it wouldn't be a danger to Callie, until he finally heard the bedroom door open.

His head swiveled, long tawny hair nearly slapping him in the cheek with how quick he turned. He hopped to his feet when he saw Louise standing in the doorway.

The midwife was smiling at him. "Congratulations, Daddy. It's a girl."

A breath caught in his throat.

A girl.

A daughter.

And quite possibly the halfling spoken of in the Shadow Prophecy...

"Come on in," Louise continued in her soft voice. "She's asking for you."

Ash was already striding for the door before she even finished her sentence.

As he approached her, he waved his hand, ready to compel her to leave the apartment and forget ever meeting them. After all, once he was done with her, he would do the same.

Except that was how Aislinn would react. The

Light Fae. The member of the Fae Queen's elite guard. He would use the human, then discard her once he had no need for her.

But Ash... Callie's Ash... he paused.

Then, because he was sure his mate would want him to, he gestured for Louise to wait. He had a roll of human money in his pants pocket. He started to peel off a few bills, hesitated again, then handed the whole roll to Louise before sending her on her way.

He didn't say 'thank you'—old habits died hard, it seemed, and Ash would forever be fae—but he was sure the midwife would much prefer the money anyway.

Once she was gone, the door closed behind her, Ash slipped into the bedroom. Part of the preparations Ash had made was bringing a second, smaller bed into the space. Like they planned, Callie had moved to it while she was in labor. Now, cleaned up and wearing a simple nightdress that, to Ash, was more beautiful than any of Melisandre's elaborate gowns, she was propped up against a wall of pillows, cradling the baby against her chest as if afraid to let her out of her sight.

He could sense her exhaustion, but there was a steely determination in her blue eyes as Callie spared him a quick glance. "They'll come for her. Won't they, Ash?"

He was fae. He couldn't lie. And even if he *could*? When it came to Callie, he wouldn't.

So, in the name of Oberon, he wished he could say otherwise, he nodded. "Yes."

"The queen... she won't stop until she has her."

That was also true. But, watching as his beloved *ffrindau* cradled their child to her chest, Ash made a solemn vow to both Callie and their daughter.

"Melisandre can try. But I won't let her."

It was the truth. At least, Ash believed it to be. For the next year, he was sure he could protect Callie and Zella, even when he could no longer deny that she *was* the halfling child spoken of in the prophecy.

Half human. Half fae. Drawn to the shadows, even though she carried Seelie blood in her veins... Zella was the only threat to the Fae Queen in two hundred years, and all too soon, Melisandre finally went after her.

And Ash was right. He didn't let her get to Zella. Neither did Callie.

If only they could've saved themselves, though...

EPILOGUE

Twenty-two years later

The world was so very different these days, thought Callie as she walked around the apartment, absently straightening up while Ash—cloaked in glamour as always—went down the street for a pepperoni pizza.

She had to admit that the changes were to be expected. Even though she still looked like, felt like, acted like she was twenty-four years old, more than two decades had passed while Callie and Ash were frozen as statues in Faerie courtesy of Melisandre's revenge. Two decades where the world turned, life went on, things changed... and her baby girl grew up.

Zella—who went by Riley, though Callie couldn't help but use her given name if only in her thoughts—

was twenty-one now, though after a lifetime of loss and tragedy, she often seemed older than she was. With the same white-blonde hair as Callie, the same blue eyes, they could pass for sisters, though sometimes Callie thought Zella acted more like the parent than she did.

From little things, like explaining to Callie and Ash how much had changed while they were trapped in Faerie, to big things like breaking them out of Melisandre's castle and using her shadow magic to bring them back to the human world, Zella was no longer the baby that Callie and Ash had been willing to sacrifice *everything* to protect.

Instead, she was a determined young woman with a mate of her own. Ninetroir, Ash's fellow guard and the Dark Fae who once owed him a life debt, turned out to be more than the protector that Callie begged and pleaded and bargained with him to be. He was Zella's fated *ffrindau*, and in the months since Zella freed Callie and Ash from their fate before following her own and facing off against Melisandre, he was as devoted to Callie's daughter as Ash still proved to be to Callie.

Case in point: though she was capable of picking up a pizza herself, Ash insisted on retrieving it for her.

Once upon a time she would've rolled her eyes at his tendency to be so overprotective. But that was the old Callie. The innocent yet stubborn girl who refused to bend for her fated mate.

That was another thing that changed, wasn't it? Ever since she returned to the human world, she struggled to regain her self-confidence. Zella was a godsend, and she didn't know what she would do without Ash, but Callie had a hard time comparing the Newport she'd lived in with a newborn to the urban center it turned into over the last twenty years. The apartment building they once lived in was now condemned, which technically made them squatters, but while they were adjusting—during the time when Ash was training Zella for her inevitable confrontation with Melisandre—Callie was happy to stay in the familiar apartment.

After Zella and Ninetroir returned from that last trip to Faerie with the news that Melisandre was dead, Callie realized that hiding in the old, warded apartment wasn't necessary anymore. Neither was constantly looking over her shoulder, worried that a fae soldier would sneak up on them at any given moment.

Not again.

Her past was gone. She lost her old life the moment Ash stabbed the fake Mitch all those years ago. She could've sworn she didn't have a future, either, not after the first time the Fae Queen's soldiers tracked her and Ash down to Newport.

But she had one now. Zella pointed that out to her. So did Ash.

She... she could still be a photographer, she supposed, though it would be a learning curve since everything was digital now.

Digital... considering mortals carried their computers around in their pockets in the shape of smartphones while Callie hadn't even had a mobile phone of her own back then, she shouldn't be surprised that her career turned digital.

Buster's was a relic of a time lost. Buster himself was in his seventies now, and according to her daughter's research, happily retired and living with his grandkids down in Georgia. He actually shut down his photo business within a few years of Callie's sudden disappearance, and though she mourned its closure the same way she mourned a lot about her old life, she was at least happy to know that Buster was still alive.

Zella had explained how nearly everyone and everything could be discovered on the internet. To Callie, who'd been graduating high school in the time when the internet belonged to rich kids, who never outgrew her habit of visiting a library, she finally understood how different her world must have seemed to Ash when they first met.

Instead of magic, though, technology ruled. In a way, Callie was grateful that computers weren't as big a deal when she was Zella's age. Thought her parents and her family would have missed her, her disappearance was more a blip than anything else.

Of course, then Zella just had to show Callie the footage captured by security cameras the day that the Fae Queen sent her soldiers after Ash and Callie and their baby. She was grateful that she wasn't recognized, if only for her poor family's sake.

When she made her deal with Ninetroir all those years ago, she'd been in a small town she now knew was called Black Pine. Five hours away from Newport where she had lived with Ash for more than a year, no one ever realized that the pretty blonde who lived with her family in Newport was the same distraught mother caught on tape abandoning her baby.

Only she hadn't abandoned Zella. Running on a fatalistic cocktail of adrenaline, recklessness, and fear, for the first time in Callie's life, her sight failed her. When met with a young man wearing a baseball hat and coveralls bearing the gas station's name, she never noticed what he was hiding beneath the brim of his cap.

He had been a Light Fae, another of Melisandre's prized guards, and the Seelie who ambushed Callie in the bathroom and dragged her through a fiery portal straight to the Fae Queen's throne room.

His name was Rysdan, she discovered when Ash ordered the other Light Fae to release her. Her mate had been overpowered by the soldiers Melisandre sent to their apartment and brought to Faerie, just like Callie, and though he struggled in his crystal cuffs when he realized that she had also been captured, he was too weak to command the other fae to do anything but smirk as he bowed before the queen.

She'd been furious when she realized that Rysdan brought Callie—but no baby. So furious, in fact, that the gasps and whispers that broke out among the crowd of fae nobles told Callie that she wasn't the only one who could see through Melisandre's glamour in that moment. It dropped for a moment while Rysdan explained that he was unable to take the baby, twisting his words expertly without ever once mentioning the deal Callie had made with Ninetroir.

Of course, she'd learned that the Light Fae had ulterior motives of his own. He'd decided to claim Zella as his own, terrorizing Callie's daughter for years while she paid the price of challenging the Fae Queen: twenty plus years had passed in the Iron while Callie stood next to her mate, frozen and unaware, just another pair of tortured statues in Melisandre's garden.

She didn't have any memories of the lost time. The last thing Callie remembered was Melisandre's eerily beautiful face smiling at her as she used her magic to turn Callie to stone when, suddenly, she was looking at a frantic female who could've been her twin.

Not her twin, though. Her daughter.

Just then, Callie missed her. Though Zella and Ninetroir had made a room of their own since their mating, she loved having her daughter near. Even if Ash was still bothered by his former comrade mating his child, they both had to realize that Zella had grown into a strong, independent woman while they were gone. She was their daughter, yeah, but she was also Ninetroir's mate, and as Callie knew, that was a bond nothing could break.

It wasn't a normal mother-daughter relationship, but Callie at least had a friend in Zella. Having her living just a floor below helped cement their growing bond, and she missed her when she was gone.

Like now. Only a few days ago, Zella and Ninetroir left for a return to Faerie. With Oberon back on the throne again, he sent Helix to bring the newly mated pair to him for... it wasn't a favor. If anyone knew that the fae didn't do favors, it was Callie. But, hell. It was a favor even if Ash or Zella or even the Summer King himself wouldn't call it that.

She didn't know when she would come back, though she swore she would once she took care of something for Oberon. With Ninetroir tagging along, Zella's personal shadow, Callie didn't worry that anything bad would happen to her daughter. But she missed her, and wished she could've had the chance to talk to her again before she left so suddenly if only because she wanted to confess her suspicions to someone and, apart from Ash, Zella was all she had.

That was her fault, too. She'd made that choice,

just like she made the choice to keep her suspicions to herself until she was able to confirm them...

Though Zella had offered to use the internet to look up Callie's family—her mother, her father, her sisters—Callie had refused. How would she explain where she'd been these last twenty-two years? Or the fact that she hadn't aged? No. Maybe one day she would, but for now... she had a new family, one she'd chosen that fateful day when she took Ash back.

And, nervously patting the closest pillow as she waited for Ash to return to the apartment with his favorite human food, it was only getting bigger...

After Zella brought them back to the Iron, it had taken him a few days to recover from her potent shadow magic. Though she was half Light Fae, half human, the Shadow Prophecy left her with the ability to manipulate shadows, something Callie figured out shortly after her birth. Zella *was* Shadow, and she had to learn that, while it made her the perfect mate for her Dark Fae, it only sickened her father.

The iron, too, Callie knew. With Melisandre still a threat, Ash pushed himself to regain as much strength as he could, even as he adjusted to the new world much quicker than Callie. Of course he did. To her three hundred-year-old lover, twenty years passing in the Iron was nothing.

To Callie, it was everything.

Still. She had a second chance.

Cradling the barely-there swell at the bottom of her belly, she thought of the pregnancy test she bought weeks ago on a hunch, but only took twenty minutes ago after Ash had set out to pick up lunch.

They had a second chance, and she looked forward to spending every bit of forever with her bonded mate.

As nervous as she was, Callie smiled. It was shaky, but sure.

Her old life was as far away as if she was still existing on the other side of the veil. Her daughter was grown, but she was safe and, with Ninetroir, in good hands. And Ash...

When he opened the door a few minutes later, holding the pizza box steadily on the palm of one hand, a bouquet of flowers tucked under his arm as he closed the door behind him, Callie's smile widened when his sun-colored eyes tracked unerringly to the way she was holding her belly.

And he knew. Without her having to say a word, she was absolutely positive that he knew.

"Calliope?"

The way he murmured her true name always did something to her. And though she had wanted to tell him explicitly that he was going to be a father again, she found herself dazzled as always when that beautiful, beautiful face locked on her.

So she just nodded, giggling when Ash dropped the pizza and the flowers where he stood before gliding over to her, swooping her up in his arms as his warmth enveloped her securely, careful not to jostle her or squeeze her too tight.

"I love you," he told her, speaking the words that never failed to mean so much if only because it was so very unlike a fae to say. But Ash wasn't just a fae—he was hers, and he always would be. "I love you so much, even more than the moon and stars put together."

Her heart full, Callie hugged him tightly as her gaze landed on the bouquet of flowers before the happy tears made her impressive sight glossy.

They had yellow blooms, as always.

Freesia.

"I love you, too, Aislinn," she whispered back.

Unconditionally.

A NOTE FROM JESSICA

Welp. There we are. The second half of the **Wanted by the Fae** duet. While the first book—Glamour Eyes—ended with Ash rejecting Callie, this book brought them back together... at least until the events of Favor, and everything that happens in my **By the Fae** universe after that.

My goal with this pair of novellas was to shed some light on Ash and Callie. In the **Touched by the Fae** series, they're important because they're Riley's parents, but now you guys can see what led them to that pivotal moment in Favor when Melisandre sent her guards after the bonded pair. And though they're no longer at the mercy of the Fae Queen when Riley's story ended, I wanted to take their HFN and turn it into a true HEA.

Hopefully, Glamour Lies did just that. I also want

to note that it's the final book in the main **By the Fae** universe. It brings the series—encompassing four short stories, two novellas, and six novels—to a close, finishing up Riley & Nine, Elle & Rys, and Callie & Ash's stories. I do plan on eventually returning to Faerie to focus on the war brewing between the Summer and Winter Courts, telling the story of Jim & Morgan, plus Branwen, Saxon, and the leader of the Wild Hunt... but that won't be for a little while yet. It could be next year, or the year after, but when we do go back to Faerie, some of the other characters will definitely make another reappearance.

After all, I'm sure you want to hear all about Riley finding out she's going to be a big sister ;)

For now, here's a sneak peek at another PNR portal fantasy novel I have coming soon. If you enjoyed Faerie, you'll love the Other, where the Greek gods and goddesses are trapped by magic to relive out their myths in newer, more modern incarnations.

xoxo,
Jessica

CHASE THE BEAUTY

The giant drops low before setting a plate of steaming food in front of me. Rising, he nudges it closer to where I'm curled up on the ground. He moves quickly for a man of his size, the light silhouetting him as he's careful to keep his big bulk to the shadows.

"For you," he says gruffly.

In the firelight, I can't tell what's loaded on it. The ceramic clinks, then scrapes against the floor of the cave as he moves it closer to me, but all I really see are shadowy lumps piled high. No. That's not all. There are wisps of smoke rising over the mounds, vanishing into the flickering flames in the grate opposite of me.

When he realized that the cave was too chilly for me, that I craved the warmth of the fire, he wordlessly shifted my furs so that I was nearer to the flames without a second warning. He already thinks I'm fragile and weak—not like I'm going to deny that—but at least he doesn't think I'm going to fall face first into the fire anymore.

I glance down at the plate. This isn't the first time he's brought me a meal, but it's been broth and bread and that jerky stuff from before. Utensils weren't necessary when I could sip the broth or tear the bread apart with my fingers.

The hot plate? Whatever it is, I don't think I'm supposed to use my hands to grab it. Then again, I don't see a fork. Is there one? I squint, but even though I've adapted to the gloom in the cave as best I can since yesterday, it's still too dark.

It's on purpose. I know it is. Though I've gotten a few glimpses of my savior since he rescued me, he seems to prefer hiding in the shadows and the darkness of his mountain sanctuary. Considering how I've learned to protect myself by doing the same thing, I can't blame him.

I also can't bring myself to be an even bigger nuisance by asking for a fork.

It's okay. I wasn't really hungry anyway.

I stay where I am while he moves to the other side of his... what did he call it? His forge? He moves to the other side of his forge while I huddle under my furs, watching as the wisps of smoke fade away as the food cools. Maybe once it's not so hot, I can use my fingers without burning the tips.

It's an idea, anyway.

The giant busies himself for a few minutes—I can't see what he's doing, but I hear the clanging of steel, wincing when it rings out over the crackle of the hungry fire—before I can sense him moving closer to me again. I already know that his sight is loads better than mine, especially in the gloom of the cave, but I guess it's even better than I thought since he can easily tell that I haven't made a move toward the plate.

"Eat," he says, his gruff voice a command that has me stiffening. He huffs, as if he saw my reaction and isn't too happy with it. "You need meat," he tells me. "You're too skinny by half, lass."

His words feel like a slap no matter how softly he mutters them or how strangely intriguing his Irish accent sounds to me. Troy likes skinny. He always has. And not just skinny, either, but an almost unattainable figure that was his ideal fantasy woman. If I so much as gained an ounce, he knew and I sure as hell paid for it. I can't count the number of nights I went to bed hungry to shave off a few calories.

Is that what I was doing now? I... I don't know.

One thing for sure? This giant of a man wants me to eat—so I do.

Gripping the nearest piece of lukewarm food with my fingers, I hope it's something recognizable before I pop it in my mouth and obediently begin to chew. It's definitely meat, with a leanness that makes me think its pork—or something close to it—and it's not bad. A little charred, but definitely edible.

He's still watching me. I swallow, then grab another piece.

Something rumbles. It takes me a second to realize that the sound is coming from him.

"What are you doin'?" he asks me.

I quickly swallow again, folding my fingers in so that I don't give in to the urge to wipe the grease from the meat on the furs he gave me. What am I doing?

My voice is quiet and a little bit confused as I admit, "What you told me to. I'm eating."

With a snort, he says, "Do you always do what you're told?"

Good question. Once upon a time, that would've been a 'no'. But Troy knocked most of my defiance out of me a long time ago, and only my sense of self preservation gave me the nerve to escape him.

To stay safe from my ex, I need this stranger to want to protect me. In order to do that, I need to keep him happy. He wants me to eat? I'll eat. I'll do anything he wants me to.

"If that's what you want me to do."

"Let's make one thing clear, lassie. I only want you to do what you want. Understand?"

I shrug.

He huffs. "Another way, then. You hungry, girl?"

I think of the barely touched plate of meat and how

Troy would hate it if I gorged myself on it. And, you know what? I *am* hungry. Now that I've just dug in and used my fingers to eat the food, any last vestiges of pride are gone—and that's assuming I had any after I fainted in front of this stranger.

I nod.

"Then eat."

Almost mechanically, I react to his soft command by grabbing another piece of meat with my fingers and bringing it to my mouth.

To my surprise, he suddenly curses under his breath in a language I've never heard before; harsh yet lyrical, there's no doubt it's profanity. I immediately stop chewing, sure that I've done something to piss him off. Great. Stuck in this unfamiliar place, hiding from Troy... he was my only hope and I've made him angry even after doing everything I could not to.

I force myself to swallow before quickly saying, "I—"

Before I can finish my hurried apology, the big man slips back into the shadows. Seconds later, he moves to the edge of the firelight, holding out one of his massive hands. The flames reflect off of something shiny. My heart leaps into my throat, my stomach churning as I think, *"knife,"* before he spins the item between those thick fingers of his.

"My fault," he says gruffly. "Shoulda remembered the damn fork."

Because that's what it is. A beautifully crafted metal fork that, no doubt, came from his forge.

My hand is shaking as I reach for it. "Thank you."

He clumsily shoves the handle against my fingers. "I shoulda remembered," is all he says again before he disappears.

There's a pit in my stomach as I glance down at my plate. I'm hungry, I have a fork, and he's purposely left me alone.

Do what I want, huh?

I stab the fork into the nearest hunk of meat, twirling it as I admit that I'm not just hungry. I'm nervous, I'm queasy, I'm scared out of my damn mind —but I'm also starving and I need to keep up my strength in case I need to escape again.

Do what I want?

Okay, then.

I'll... I'll try.

Vanessa

I always told myself that I would get out when I finally had enough. After four years of an emotionally abusive relationship, I was beginning to think that I'd let him control me forever. Besides, he only ever got violent once before. And I believed him when he swore he didn't mean it.

Then came the night when he... he *snapped*. In a haze of fury, he attacked me with a knife and I finally found the strength to fight back. Leaving him for dead, I grabbed my keys and ran.

I've been running ever since.

He found me, just like I knew he would—because I didn't kill him, though I know he'll kill me the second he gets the chance. He found me, and there was nowhere left to run—so, instead, I jumped. Through an antique mirror and into a world I never even dreamed existed.

I ran right into the biggest, baddest man I'd ever seen.

And, for the first time in years, I'm safe.

***

Hephaestus

They told me she would come. I told them I didn't care.

I lied. Oh, did I lie.

The story always ends the same. It doesn't matter that she is lost and lonely, quiet and scared—*scarred*. She's not meant to be mine. My beauty, my Aphrodite, could never love a monster like me.

***

Troy

Vanessa is mine. And I will move Heaven or Earth —or jump into a whole other world—to bring her back home where she belongs.

So what if she's the one who ran away? Or that

she's found some big shot to take care of her in the time since she's been gone? I'll get her back.

Even if we have to go to war.

Chase the Beauty is the sixth entry in the *Mirrorside* series. It's a twist on the myths featuring both Aphrodite/Hephaestus & Aphrodite/Ares, with a goddess of love who doesn't believe in the stuff and the gentle giant Hef getting the HEA he's long been denied.

Coming January 18, 2022

STAY IN TOUCH

Interested in updates from me? I'll never spam you, and I'll only send out a newsletter in regards to upcoming releases, subscriber exclusives, promotions, and more:

Sign up for my newsletter here!

For a limited time, anyone who signs up for my newsletter will also receive two free books!

ABOUT THE AUTHOR

Jessica lives in New Jersey with her family, including enough pets to cement her status as the neighborhood's future Cat Lady. She spends her days working in retail, and her nights lost in whatever world the current novel she is working on is set in. After writing for fun for more than a decade, she has finally decided to take some of the stories out of her head and put them out there for others who might also enjoy them! She loves Broadway and the Mets, as well as reading in her free time.

JessicaLynchWrites.com
jessica@jessicalynchwrites.com

ALSO BY JESSICA LYNCH

Welcome to Hamlet

You Were Made For Me*

Don't Trust Me

Ophelia

Let Nothing You Dismay

I'll Never Stop

Wherever You Go

Here Comes the Bride

Gloria

Tesoro

Holly

That Girl Will Never Be Mine

Welcome to Hamlet: I-III**

No Outsiders Allowed: IV-VI**

Mirrorside

Tame the Spark*

Stalk the Moon

Hunt the Stars

The Witch in the Woods

Hide from the Heart

Chase the Beauty

Flee the Sun

The Other Duet**

The Claws Clause

Mates*

Hungry Like a Wolf

Of Mistletoe and Mating

No Way

Season of the Witch

Rogue

Sunglasses at Night

Ghost of Jealousy

Broken Wings

Born to Run

Uptown Girl

Ordinance 7304: I-III**

Living on a Prayer**

The Curse of the Othersiders

(Part of the Claws Clause Series)

Ain't No Angel*

True Angel

Night Angel

Lost Angel

Touched by the Fae

Favor*

Asylum

Shadow

Touch

Zella

The Shadow Prophecy**

Imprisoned by the Fae

Tricked*

Trapped

Escaped

Freed

Gifted

The Shadow Realm**

Wanted by the Fae

Glamour Eyes

Glamour Lies

Forged in Twilight

House of Cards

Ace of Spades

Royal Flush

Claws and Fangs

(written under Sarah Spade)

Leave Janelle*

Never His Mate

Always Her Mate

Forever Mates

Hint of Her Blood

* prequel story

** boxed set collection

Printed in Great Britain
by Amazon